Praise for *Let There Be Blood*

"An intriguing Byronic hero in this first of a new series with stylistic overtones evocative of the Brontë sisters . . . full of surprises, revealing hidden depths . . . The carefully constructed plot provides an illuminating glimpse of the years between the self-indulgence of the Regency and the rigid propriety of the Victorians." —*Publishers Weekly*

"Excellent prose, solid characterization, and authentic period atmosphere." —*Library Journal*

"An exciting historical mystery." —*Midwest Book Review*

"Lord Ambrose is a fanciable mixture of Byron and Mr. Rochester . . . This series is going to be a winner."
—Veronica Stallwood

"This mystery has a charm that grows upon the reader. It works because it's cleverly executed." —*Yorkshire Post*

"Sophisticated and stylish . . . dark and labyrinthine . . . Jane Jakeman takes us on a thrilling roller coaster of unpredictable yet believable twists and turns." —*Historical Novels Review*

"Lovely stuff, wreathed round by the olde-worlde atmosphere of intrepid derring-do." —*The Irish Times*

In the Kingdom of Mists

"Jakeman expertly captures the atmosphere of England . . . A chilling historical police procedural." —*Midwest Book Review*

"Intelligent . . . an absolute must for all devotees of historical crime fiction." —*The Times* (London)

continued . . .

"Jakeman offers Monet's misty vision as a wonderfully astute way of revealing the mysteries of London." —*The Independent*

"Combines the dramatic tension of a crime thriller with the lyricism of the art world . . . Jakeman's clever interweaving of the characters makes for an enjoyable read." —*Hello!*

"Jakeman writes intelligently about art and artists and throws in a crackingly atmospheric historical thriller to boot." —*The Birmingham Post*

"A dramatic story about crime and perception, art and reality . . . Multi-layered and -voiced, this is a fascinating attempt to add an extra dimension to the historical crime novel." —*Guardian*

"Monet's elusive and vivid canvases color the whole narrative, lending an eerie sheen . . . The plot has drive and is choreographed neatly, and the evocation of the period is excellent." —*Scotland on Sunday*

"A great read—the stark contrast between the beautiful descriptions of Monet's paintings and the macabre murders held my attention to the very last page." —Janet Gleeson

"A lovely novel—compulsively readable and beautifully written." —Colin Dexter

"Vivid . . . The author convincingly evokes fin-de-siècle London with its class and gender prejudices." —*Publishers Weekly*

"A neatly plotted, finely phrased tale, full of period atmosphere." —*Booklist*

FOOL'S GOLD

By Jane Jakeman

IN THE KINGDOM OF MISTS

The Lord Ambrose Mysteries

LET THERE BE BLOOD

THE EGYPTIAN COFFIN

FOOL'S GOLD

FOOL'S GOLD

JANE JAKEMAN

BERKLEY PRIME CRIME, NEW YORK

THE BERKLEY PUBLISHING GROUP
Published by the Penguin Group
Penguin Group (USA) Inc.
375 Hudson Street, New York, New York 10014, USA
Penguin Group (Canada), 90 Eglinton Avenue East, Suite 700, Toronto, Ontario M4P 2Y3, Canada
(a division of Pearson Penguin Canada Inc.)
Penguin Books Ltd., 80 Strand, London WC2R 0RL, England
Penguin Group Ireland, 25 St. Stephen's Green, Dublin 2, Ireland (a division of Penguin Books Ltd.)
Penguin Group (Australia), 250 Camberwell Road, Camberwell, Victoria 3124, Australia
(a division of Pearson Australia Group Pty. Ltd.)
Penguin Books India Pvt. Ltd., 11 Community Centre, Panchsheel Park, New Delhi—110 017, India
Penguin Group (NZ), Cnr. Airborne and Rosedale Roads, Albany, Auckland 1310, New Zealand
(a division of Pearson New Zealand Ltd.)
Penguin Books (South Africa) (Pty.) Ltd., 24 Sturdee Avenue, Rosebank, Johannesburg 2196, South Africa

Penguin Books Ltd., Registered Offices: 80 Strand, London WC2R 0RL, England

PRINTING HISTORY
Headline Book Publishing edition / 1998
Headline Book Publishing paperback edition / 1999
Berkley Prime Crime trade paperback edition / February 2006

Library of Congress Cataloging-in-Publication Data

Jakeman, Jane.
Fool's gold / by Jane Jakeman.
p. cm.
ISBN 0-425-20777-3
1. Malfine, Ambrose, Lord (Fictitious character)—Fiction. 2. Physicians—Crimes against—Fiction. 3. Aristocracy (Social class)—Fiction. 4. West Country (England)—Fiction. 5. Governesses—Fiction. I. Title.

PR6060.A435F66 2006
823'.92—dc22

2005045396

PRINTED IN THE UNITED STATES OF AMERICA

10 9 8 7 6 5 4 3 2 1

For J. M. as always.
And with great gratitude to Teresa C.
And to a real-life Arabian foal,
Zaraband Bint Nikita.

Part One

MAY, 1833

CHAPTER 1

I feared for Elisabeth, even before I got her first letter from Jesmond Place. I should have known then that a mad but cunning mind was at work, systematically, carefully, in a determined pursuit, willing to destroy everything and everyone in its way.

Yet the train of events which was to lead to two deaths, and to an accusation of murder against an innocent woman, had begun much earlier, even before I proposed to open up the abandoned ballroom in my own house, Malfine.

My mother, Eurydice, had died some twenty years previously. My father, apparently a stolid Englishman, had died also, having departed from his role as local squire and overseer of that tedious daily chronicle of trivia which some people account such a charming feature of country life. Quite suddenly after my mother's death, he began to behave like the protagonist of a Greek tragedy, something wild, absurd, yet pitiable. The comparison with a tragic hero is perhaps not so inappropriate as it might seem, since my mother had been Greek, and thus she represented his connection with a larger, stranger world, a world of terrible events and powerful feelings, of the kind that are not supposed even to exist in the middle of the placid English countryside.

At any rate, my mother's rooms had remained untouched since her death. Within those doors lay mementos of the past: the embroidered flounced skirts of her native Crete, the heavy velvet cloaks and corded silk dresses which my father had bought her, the gilded icons of her faith, and her fantastic jewelry made of misshapen baroque pearls and branching coral twigs, of Venetian enameling and Greek filigree.

I had never opened those rooms. Neither I nor my sister Ariadne had wished to do so. There was no shortage of money for Ariadne to have new clothes more suited to her style and youth. As for the other jewelry—the solid pieces which my father had purchased for my mother in Bond Street—the necklaces, aigrettes and bracelets set with diamonds which were suited to the wife of a rich English peer, had been placed, each piece in its own secure leather case, in the care of Messrs. Hoare until Ariadne should come of age. This event had occurred several years previously, but my sister was still abroad at the time of which I write, and the most valuable part of her portion therefore lay in the safekeeping of a London banker.

So the Greek inheritance lies shut away, except in so far as Ariadne and I carry it in our blood—I, in my dark skin and my damned rebellious disposition. In her, it is not so physically apparent; it lies perhaps deeper within, and will emerge later. At present, she is in all outward appearances a conventional English lady, traveling in the Levant with her husband.

But in our great West Country estate of Malfine, not only

my mother's apartments remained shuttered and silent. On my return from Greece, I had a few rooms made habitable—a couple of bedrooms out of the forty or so, the library, a bedchamber fitted up for my sister should she desire to stay.

Malfine's great ballroom had not been used for three decades or more. My grandfather, old Hedger, had not approved of the vast expense of such flim-flammery anyway. The house, when he bought it, came complete with a ballroom so that it might fulfill the requirements of a rich man's residence, as a gentleman's library might come furnished with the complete leather-bound works of Plutarch, so many yards of leather bindings to fill the shelves. Both ballroom and books were suitable and appropriate attachments. There was no positive requirement to dance in the one or peruse the other!

In the volumes on the library shelves at Malfine were still to be found the bookplates of the last member of the Danby family, who had ruled the district since the Middle Ages. Charles Danby, the most generous of spirits, had thought himself to be Kubla Khan and lavished everything on this house. It was his semi-fabulous castle in the air, his gorgeous earthly Jerusalem, until the dreams caved in and he sold it all, the land, the woods, the mansion itself from the white marble flight of steps at the entrance to the gilded lightning-conductors on the roof. He sold it cheap, for it was a forced sale, to my grandfather. The magnificent ballroom had just been completed, one of the greatest in the entire West Country, but my grandfather Hedger—this, you will gather, took place before the day when my family became ennobled—old Hedger, I say, had no desire for gallivanting about the floor cocking up first one leg and then the other, as he put it.

But he never let anything go to waste or rack and ruin: one of his maxims was to always hold on to what you have. I know this is not a very elegant nor a well-turned phrase, and I daresay that there are many splendid heraldic mottoes which he might have had emblazoned on the shield which he purchased, but mere heraldry does not build houses, nor keep them standing, neither. So Hedger inspected his ballroom, and pronounced it fit for nincompoops yet an investment for his heirs.

I think he had in mind both the gorgeous furnishings of the ballroom and the splendid setting it would provide for a great occasion—for entertaining royalty, say. And though he did not want to give any immediate opportunity for dancing and prancing, he always protected his investments. So he ordered special covers for the magnificent sprung parquet floor of fir and walnut, over which the Danbys and their friends had twirled in rose and almond silks. And overhead, above this dull baize covering, the Murano chandeliers, their glittering drops and links intricately assembled by Italian craftsmen who had traveled with them, hung swathed in canvas wrappers like great cocoons awaiting the hatching of some fantastic insects.

My father had three or four times ordered the floor-covers rolled back, engaged musicians and cooks and torch-bearers, and given a ball for all the county, but these were rare occasions even during my mother's lifetime. She was a shy, retiring woman, nervous of her English neighbors, and after her death, there were no more entertainments at Malfine.

As for myself, I had returned from my ventures in Greece and withdrew into a kind of inner hermitage, hiding away in the great house like an animal that licks its wounds. Gradually however, the world outside had got some of its tentacles into my lair. Humanity began to impinge. My manservant, Belos, lived in the house. There was the groom who slept above the stables. And then, with the affair of the murders at Crawshay's farmhouse, I had found myself inextricably entangled with life. Into the void came Elisabeth, brought out of that savage family to the safety of Malfine, and with her the child, Edmund Crawshay, to whom she had been governess. His parents were now dead and he had no one else in the world.

This was our household at the start of this story. But I became aware that the freedom of passion which had been the rallying cry and watchword of my youth had been restrained by iron social regimentations which were descending upon us. The conventions of proper society were threatening our lives.

I obeyed convention in one respect: I sent the child to school, and he was happy there, which I found strange, yet he wished for no more than to do as his fellows, to play their games and dash about at their sports. A sad little fellow, yet there seemed nothing else that he desired—at least, nothing that could be got in this world.

So far, at any rate, I had done what society required of me and more: I had fulfilled neighborly obligations to young Edmund and ensured that he should be educated according to the status of a gentleman. But with Elisabeth, the case was different. With Miss Elisabeth Anstruther, I found myself struck for the first time in my life by a curious kind of helplessness engendered by passion: I was smitten by that woman when first I clapped eyes on her, and could not free myself no matter how I tried—and the same seemed to hold true for her. Only, I was never sure of it.

So we were linked together, like two birds on a chain.

First one and then the other tried to find liberty, only to come fluttering lamely home again.

It was in the great ballroom that we stood, Elisabeth and I, one early May morning. There was a pale yellow light, the cruel sunshine that exposes all complexions and all scars. The thick baize covering was still over the floor, muffling our steps as we walked across it. The sunlight now revealed shredding painted wallpaper, the slimy brownish tracks of rain-deluges over gilded plasterwork, the cobwebs and scuttling spiders on the heavy shutters which I had just pulled back.

Our voices echoed beneath the domed ceiling. I remember them clearly—the dying drifts of sound, echoing into the height above us, and the words that we spoke. I remember them most clearly, for I was proposing marriage.

And suffering rejection. A most unusual experience for me, for I was not much accustomed to refusal, although admittedly it had never before been marriage that I had proposed.

"I brought you to this room," I began, "because I wanted to ask you, in this place. Here you can see what I can give you—and what it would demand of you. If you wish, we can re-open the ballroom, re-gild the lily, re-silver the mirrors—and you would be the mistress of it, as of the rest of Malfine. I wish to offer you marriage, Elisabeth, and I must also offer you the life which honorably accompanies it."

She looked at me with her yellow eyes, her gaze catching directly into mine. She had always a remarkable directness of speech, as of gaze: it was what I had most admired about her when first we met, that and the bold sensuality of her strong, tall body and her pale face, with those topaz eyes, set perhaps almost too close together so that her face had a strange, narrow look.

"Ambrose, you have lived out of the ways of the world since your return from Greece. Your wounds have healed, yet still you do not rejoin society, indeed, I believe you will never wish to do so. Perhaps it is because of your natural temperament, or perhaps your Greek blood alienates you from our ways. At all events, the last thing I would ask of you is that you should sacrifice your solitary way of life for an existence which you would find hateful—the country squire who must play host to all comers. Yes, in many ways I naturally desire to be your wife, that I freely admit, for there is no false pride between us. Yet I will never allow you to sacrifice yourself to marriage—for I perceive that you need your solitude still, and to marry is to step out and declare yourself joined with another being, in front of all the world, is it not?"

"But I wish to take that step!"

"No, not when you consider what may probably follow. Can you resign yourself to receiving the county families, to opening the house up for our children, for all the hundred and one social occasions that familial life would necessarily entail?"

"I wish to attempt it, for your sake."

"And grow to hate me, as some Lady Lummocking pours tales of the parish pump into your ear and you fret to be in your library or the stables—or more probably to go again across the seas to some alien land!"

"And fight again for a hopeless cause, you would say!"

"Well, is it not true?"

I was silent, loosening her long chestnut hair that I loved to caress. I remember exactly how it felt, springing with life as it curled down beneath my fingertips.

I had to admit that I might never be free of a certain contagion, an infection for liberty, with which precious few Englishmen are afflicted. English society is in some ways anathema to me; the requirement to bow the knee to some dull and sozzled monarch, to mouth allegiance to a row of coronetted turnips, to chant along with my neighbors some applications for the safety of a crown for which I cared very little, addressing those prayers to an Almighty for Whom I cared even less—these mindless customs had always revolted me. Try though I would to suffer them for my Elisabeth's sake, yet I knew that rebellion might break out within my imprisoned soul if it were "cabined, cribbed, confined."

In any case, she spoke very decisively at that time.

"Ambrose, I will not have you, for your own sake. I will not cage you, to lead a life you do not desire in your heart, but which you will feel you must give me. And besides, there is another matter . . ."

"If you are going to speak again of the difference—"

"In our rank and wealth? Yes, I must speak of it, for you cannot pretend that it does not exist. How can you have, as a fit consort to rule this great house, a woman who has been a servant herself, who has been a penniless governess in a farmhouse? These things count for much in English society and cannot be easily set aside. There would be whispering and murmuring for the rest of our lives, behind our backs—and what of our children? Will people not say that it is all very well, that they are heirs to a great estate, but their mother was the daughter of a wine merchant—and mixed up in a most dubious scandal!"

"Let them say it. There is no cause for shame in any of it."

"Yet you cannot persuade me that the views of the world count for nothing. I will, indeed I *must,* refuse you."

I will not dwell on this scene.

It was not the end of the matter. We might have continued as we were, living in a few rooms in the great mansion of Malfine, with the great suite in which my mother had been installed still shut off. But we were to plunge deeper into the frets of living, into the tangling mesh and snarled wires of thought and feeling which communication with the outside world inevitably brings in its wake.

The background to all this, the circumstances of Elisabeth's removal to Jesmond Place, I must briefly sketch. The history which will be revealed in the following papers is now part of our story and that of Malfine itself. Yet it is a secret history: if some pious future age comes to marvel at this house and tell its story, our dead fears and passions will lie crumbling in some attic.

For the present, this account of the real nature of certain events shall suffice. I say "the real nature of events"—I mean, the vile truth behind them.

At the time, I begged Elisabeth not to go.

I confess that this was no display of foresight as to the terrible enactments that were to occur at Jesmond Place, but rather the result of my own selfishness and my reluctance to give her up. Yet her insistence prevailed over mine, and at the time it seemed entirely right that it should. "I cannot and will not cling and fawn upon you," she said. "I have always had a proud and independent spirit and would think it shame to soak up your wealth as if I were a sea-sponge!"

"Dear Elisabeth," I replied—we were now on the lawn under the cedar trees planted before Malfine was built, by that noble idiot who frivolled away all his wealth—"Dear Elisabeth, I find myself appallingly well-furnished! I am in the process of allowing my ancestral mansion to fall to bits, and have no extravagances except our small household and the maintenance of our stables. Edmund is no drain on my purse save for his school fees and a modest supply of bug-bottles; you refuse to accept any gifts whatsoever. Apart from the compensation which I regularly have to make to my neighbors for the depredations caused by Zaraband's taste for exotic flora, I am at virtually no expense to maintain the whole pack of you. As for Belos, he is the most discreet of menservants who ever served a master, for he appears to scrutinize all my household bills through a magnifying glass before allowing me to make any payments whatsoever, and seems content with a new suit of brown velvet once a year. I beg you, stay. You have no need to go earning your living again as a governess, subject to the whim of any country numbskulls with enough money to employ a French polisher for their tiny block-heads."

Did she listen to me?

Well, what would you expect? She had already made inquiries of our neighbor, Lady Anderton. That personage had been informed that the Jesmonds, a family of quality not far distant, required some genteel female.

To Jesmond Place, then, Elisabeth wished to depart. Her natural independence of spirit asserted itself: she could, she averred, earn her bread if she was turned out of Malfine in her petticoats, a thought which briefly caused us some merriment, but she took it more seriously than I thought. Not the petticoats, but the earning of her living.

It was true that Jesmond Place appeared to offer many advantages. In fact, it was the post of companion to Lady Jesmond, and not a position as a children's governess, that was offered. This lady, it seemed, suffered from a rather solitary existence, her husband being of a studious and scholarly temperament, leaving his wife to her own devices while he remained closeted with musty instruments and arcane literature.

"And Lady Jesmond wishes me to teach her French," Elisabeth said, when we were standing on the lawn, after her first visit to the lady of the house to discuss the proposed enslavement. "I think she would prove an apt pupil. We tried a little and Lady Jesmond showed herself to have a good ear at the language; she is a quick and accurate mimic and can give me back a sound with uncanny accuracy. It is odd, though . . ."

Here, she paused as if contemplating what was strange in her new employer, tossing back a lock of hair, and continued: "The effect of my lady's speech is a trifle unusual; though she may speak with a country burr, yet she can imitate a fine gentlewoman's manner quite perfectly, if she chooses. I think that she did not have the advantage of much education of any kind when she was young, yet she speaks uncommonly well. But indeed, she is of low birth, so Lady Anderton considers it."

"Well, if Lady Jesmond is at least legitimate, that will be a living rebuke to the race of Anderton," said I, but could not deter my companion from her topic.

"It is said that Sir Antony met her when he was on a journey and was forced to take shelter in a thunderstorm. Anyway, it seems that lightning struck! She is his second wife—there is a son by the first, who died some years ago, but he, of course, is grown now; he is a student at Oxford and comes home only during the University vacations. In fact, I don't suppose he can be so many years younger than

Lady Jesmond; they are probably much of an age! She still has the freshness of youth, I thought upon meeting her, only perhaps rather run to *embonpoint.*"

"The sooner Lady Jesmond learns French, the sooner she will grasp the meaning of such delicate terms," said I. "What else does her ladyship require?"

"To learn a little music and drawing and so forth. She has never been taught the accomplishments of a lady, and I, as you know, have been instructed in little else."

"The rest of your spirit comes to you naturally, then," I observed, and dodged the book she swung at my head. "But what of Sir Antony? Does he approve this plan for educating his lady?"

"Yes, or so he said, but I confess I talked to him only for a few minutes. He seemed pleasant enough—rather distracted, I thought. He is very much older than she, I should say by twenty years or more. And they have appointed a resident physician, a young man called Kelsoe, to attend to Sir Jesmond during his rheumatic attacks. Lady Jesmond seems an amiable and good-tempered creature. The house is rather dark, but I am to have a very comfortable room with chintz hangings."

There was a pause, I having nothing to say on the subject of chintz, and no capacity at that moment for saying anything on more serious matters. Then she added, slowly, "So you see, nothing stands in the way of my going."

How I wish to Heaven I had said then and there: "Yes, *I* stand in the way—I and Malfine—we will not let you depart. Damn the chintz! Never leave!"

Of course, I said not a word.

I cannot claim any great prescience of the events that followed, for my first apprehension was only that Elisabeth might be unhappy, not that she might be in danger. Yet, later in this history, I should have understood the meaning of that scrap of paper, with those few words upon it.

Coals of fire.
Quicksilver.
Cakes of glass.

Isolation. That was another key, or so I would remember, later on. Too late.

Jesmond Place is about thirty miles west from Malfine, near a small village called Combwich. It is an odd area: dotted about with drowsy little huddles and apple orchards, yet close to the shore, washed by the high waters of the Bristol Channel which swirl inland, gushing up the creeks and rivers. At low tide, the banks of rivers and streams are smooth pillows of shining mud; at high tide, the brown seawater pours in to cover them. This gives the landscape an uncertain, unstable effect, if I may describe it so. Sometimes it is rolling rich green pasture and hedge: then round a bend in the road ahead there may suddenly glimmer a wet and glistening vista, merging in the distance into a silvery vaporous sky. The Jesmonds lived inland about three or four miles distant from the coast; their noddle-headed ancestors at least had the sense to build on rising ground.

I had ridden past the house on one or two occasions, though I had never been inside it, and had never met any of the Jesmond family. I recalled a poky, rambling old manor house, probably complete with wormholed timbering and dank little garrets: it had mouldered quietly along since before the time of old Queen Bess.

I hate dark and ancient houses. It is one of the blessings of my existence that instead of a crumbling ivy-covered mass which has stood on the spot for centuries, such as the Jesmonds inhabit, I have my present airy dominion, a rational classical mansion with clean marble stairs and great windows that flood the rooms with light. Otherwise I might have had to live in such a dismal rabbit-warren as that where Elisabeth took up residence as my lady Jesmond's companion.

I had Elisabeth's description of the Jesmonds, but wanted to know more.

"The Jesmonds were always respectable enough, though inclined to book-learning. That is the talk in the village, my lord."

Belos, my manservant, was decanting claret in my dining room, holding the blackish bottle of wine up to the light to inspect it, pouring the fluid as gently as if he were tending an infant's posset-cup, giving the glinting facets of the decanter a final polish with a silk kerchief. He is an actor who has retired from the stage, but not from life.

And could be relied upon to pick up news, for unlike myself he is afflicted with the need for human company, and occasionally passes a few hours in the village alehouse that lies just beyond the gates of Malfine.

"I did not think, Belos, that they would know anything about the Jesmonds; it is quite some distance from here."

"You would be surprised, my lord, at how news blazes about in the countryside. They are so starved for any titbits of gossip; anyone who travels the roads—the carter, the pedlar, the coachmen—they are all mobbed as soon as they come through the village. Besides, I made it my business to make some inquiries, as soon as I heard Miss Anstruther was going there. I would not like her to be entering into a household of which we knew nothing at all."

"Your concern for Miss Anstruther does you credit, Belos. But what of Lady Jesmond—do they say anything of her in the village?"

"That she was once very lovely, though now somewhat run to fat, and that she is generous. Also that she is rather neglected by her husband, who spends his days in his library, and is very much older than his lady. His rheumatic afflictions prevent him from . . . er, from riding, I understand."

"Quite so, and delicately put. Well, we must hope for the best."

This conversation took place a few days before Elisabeth left for Jesmond Place, and it had done something to reassure me as to her departure. Not only was the Jesmond household a model of respectability, so it appeared, but of excruciating dullness, and I was sufficiently vain to imagine that no woman could prefer a quiet life without me to the exotic excitements of my company. She would get bored soon enough.

Perhaps Sir Antony Jesmond was unsound, for there is always something a little dangerous about "book-learning," but in the country a few dusty shelves in a library could well lie behind such a reputation. In any case, I hardly imagined that the squire of Jesmond Place could prove a spark-striking intellectual tinderbox.

I therefore told myself that this new state of affairs whereby Elisabeth departed Malfine to live beneath the roof of some country booby could not long endure. And I made no more objections.

So it was that one chilly day in late spring the Malfine carriage, with its black coachwork polished up a little and the doors adorned by the faded gilt of my wolf's-head crest, took Elisabeth, her trunk and valises, with her paints and brushes and drawing-board packed up in one folder and her sheets of music in another, to her new abode. I had misgivings, I must confess, as I watched the carriage roll down the ruts in my weed-filled drive and observed Pellers getting out to tug the gates open from their ivy entanglements. Centered upon my own feelings as my thoughts usually are, my doubts related to the nature of her feelings toward me, and did not allow for the world outside.

When her letter arrived, therefore, I was unprepared for its tone, for the general undercurrent of distress that I sensed lay behind the calm terms with which she recorded the household and events at Jesmond Place.

That letter, to be sure, contained little that, on the surface of things, appeared likely to cause any alarm. What was it, then? "I understand," Elisabeth wrote,

> *that Dr. Kelsoe has been engaged specifically to take charge of Sir Antony's health, he having suffered much of late, not only from rheumatism and similar afflictions of* anno domini *but from shooting pains in his chest, which according to the physicians augured that all might not be well with the heart. It is about three miles to Combwich village, and there is nowhere nearer in the neighborhood. Not a good situation for an invalid, if Sir Antony should suffer some difficulties with his health. The house here being so isolated and far from help in any emergency . . .*

There! That's what it was! Those were the words that made the hairs stand up on my neck, though it was not Sir Antony's health that concerned me. Merely the knowledge that Elisabeth would be away from any assistance.

I read on, and the sensation of unease increased. I was

crumpling the edges of the paper as my eye raced along the lines.

The house here being so isolated and far from help in any emergency, it was felt that it would be well to have a resident medical man, and Dr. John Kelsoe arrived from Bristol a few months ago, to supply the want. He had not set up in independent practice, his experience deriving chiefly, it seems, from acting as locum tenens *to several medical men in Clifton.*

I heard about him from the lady of the house. "I believe, Miss Anstruther, he was thought a most brilliant young man by his professors," Lady Jesmond told me when we were sitting drinking tea one afternoon. "My husband speaks most highly of his qualifications! And the young man is willing to help Antony with his scientific papers and so forth. I trust, Miss Anstruther, that you are not hoping for a lively addition to our household, for he is a quiet-minded sort of creature who spends his evenings shut away! He told Sir Antony that he wanted to leave Bristol in order to carry out some studying for which he never had time . . . That's why Jesmond Place will suit him so well, you see. He has agreed to come very cheap . . ."

Here she paused, laughing in a little embarrassed way, no doubt wondering whether this were not too vulgar an expression, and then continued: "By that I mean for less than such a clever gentleman might expect, so that he can bury his head in his books, for that is his idea of pleasure, it seems! Well, I never thought studying did a body much good, Miss Anstruther. You cannot say it has kept my husband in good health, and I'm sure he has spent most of his life moiling over his old papers and those stinking flasks and powders!"

Her ladyship uttered a great sigh, and truly I felt much sympathy for her; the edge of her beauty is perhaps gone, faded off, but her hair is still bright, of a lively golden tone, her eye still blue and her cheek rounded and charming. Her figure is too full to please the fashionable, but she dresses well, even in the depths of the countryside. This is really one of her chief entertainments, for she delights to put on new lace, or to have a dress made up from a pattern arrived from Bath, although there are so few to make observation of her charms. As for her husband, he may see *but appears not to* care *a jot. He seldom pays his lady any compliment or little attentions, though he is always careful to be very courteous to her and correct in his address. Indeed, I noticed on one occasion that he reprimanded the housekeeper, Mrs. Romey, for presuming not to use my lady's title and taking a liberty beyond that usually permitted to a servant.*

Mrs. Romey has sometimes a kind of affectionate freedom of address, I suppose the consequence of having been so long here that she partly takes the privileges of a member of the family, and one day at tea-time when my lady did not take anything to eat, Mrs. Romey leaned over her chair and said in motherly tones, "There, my pretty, tha must keep thy strength up!" Sir Antony happening unusually to be in the room, he immediately called out to Mrs. Romey: "Kindly address her ladyship respectfully!" I confess that I was not much endeared toward him by this instance, for Mrs. Romey's remark, though perhaps a trifle familiar, was kindly meant.

Dr. Kelsoe was introduced to me at dinner, where he sat opposite on my first evening here. He is a pale man, perhaps in his early twenties, not so young as I had expected, with reddish-brown eyes, deep-set and restless. He looked about all the time, seeming to wish particularly not to look at my lady Jesmond, for he always answered her with his eyes on my face, and not on hers, where she sat at the end of the table, facing Sir Antony.

The four of us were at the dining-table—Sir Antony and Lady Jesmond, Dr. Kelsoe and myself—and to say that the conversation flagged would give an extravagantly lively picture! It was already stone dead. I struggled politely for a while with remarks about the charms of Bristol, to which Dr. K. gave no more response than the barest of polite nods and mumbles. Poor Lady Jesmond made a few frivolous requests for information about cashmere shawls which Dr. Kelsoe lately might have seen on a visit to Clifton, which received such snubbing comments from the young man as: "I fear, madam, that I do not take much consideration of such trifles." And as for Sir Antony, he said almost nothing, merely slurped his turbot soup over his skinny knees (Sir Antony is not a nice eater), and "trusted that Dr. Kelsoe would give him some advice as to which items of diet might over-heat the blood and should on that account be avoided."

Dr. Kelsoe's replies seemed modest and sensible: of the quality of his medical opinions I cannot judge, but Sir Antony pronounced himself satisfied. The young man is taciturn, or perhaps preoccupied would better fit the case, as if he were thinking of something beyond our little social pleasantries. I will not say that I find his manner to be entirely agreeable; it is too aloof and superior for my taste.

The housekeeper, Mrs. Romey, attends to all the domestic arrangements needed by this odd and diverse band of people. She is plump, pink-faced, wears a white mob-cap with the strings pulled under her chin, a very countrywoman with open countenance and careful habits. In her kitchen at Jesmond Place she presides over order and cleanliness; a great table, well scrubbed; ovens well blacked. Sometimes I have to go into the kitchen on an errand from Lady Jesmond, and Mrs. Romey is often there. She is the only servant who sleeps in the house, though there is a boy in the stables and the maids come in from the village each day.

But my letter runs on, and I turn to thoughts of you . . .

There followed some private comments of an entirely different nature, which showed me that the chilly atmosphere of the Jesmond household had not wholly overwhelmed at least one inhabitant. Cold blood, hot blood . . .

That was her first letter. Dawn was breaking when the groom brought me the second one, three weeks later. In the meantime, I had refused to fret, as much as I was able, and had ridden hard every day, galloping through the neighboring countryside to the surprise of the peasantry, who were not accustomed to see me so far from home. On that particular morning I was still at home, in the library, watching the shadows falling black and green across the lawn, fading slowly. In the distance the clumps of trees at the edge of the wood were already visible; the spring dawn was environing the house gradually, like silent, cool, silver water.

The superscription on the letter was in Elisabeth's hand. As always, I knew it in an instant, would have known it among a thousand others, will know it till my dying day.

Not pausing to light a candle though it was still shadowy, I broke the seal, letting the crumbs of red wax fall to the ground as I held the papers up to the window and read on, as the day slowly brightened.

We have endured the most frightful event and I have only now been able to retire to my room and write. I have scarce been able to leave Lady Jesmond's side.

The body was found yesterday. When I first heard the alarm raised, I apprehended of course that there was some-

thing amiss with Sir Antony, for the household has, as I mentioned in my last letter, been perturbed about his heart. Yet, sad though we would have found some final shock delivered to the master of Jesmond Place, a worse tragedy has struck, in circumstances which must create fear and suspicion and have ended a life which had scarcely begun to fill its promise.

CHAPTER 2

MY eye rushed along the lines as the early-morning sun fell on the pages of her letter.

> *Young Dr. Kelsoe was discovered lying in his own bed, a lifeless corpse. What was the cause of his death? Apparently the poor fellow was not a suicide, which makes worse the anxiety and doubt which now overshadow Jesmond Place.*
>
> *I will recount the events as briefly as I may, for I write in haste, not knowing when I may be called for to assist my lady.*
>
> *The first I knew of the tragedy was when Mrs. Romey roused me late at night—about midnight, I think—and asked me to follow her upstairs. I went at once, and heard Lady Jesmond calling out from the young man's chamber. I assumed Mrs. Romey had already summoned her. I do not know that she was saying anything in particular—it was really more of a frantic calling and crying. When I entered I found her distractedly trying to raise Dr. Kelsoe up from the bed.*

All was panic and alarm, for the body had just been discovered, or so I was told; I gently pulled Lady Jesmond away, persuading her that she could do no good there, for there seemed no signs of life in the young man whatsoever. She was sobbing and distraught, yet let herself be persuaded away from the deathbed, which I must admit was a fearful sight. He lay there in the most pitiful way—it would have broken a heart of stone to see it, his face so bluish-pale, his jaws tight-clenched. I bent over him, so close to his lifeless face that I could smell a strange odor emanating from the mouth and I could see the lips were purplish and streaked with froth. The eyes were horrible to behold, glaring, fixed, starting out of the head and with a dreadful glassy look. That face haunted my dreams last night, I must confess it!

I got my lady out of the room and down the stairs, and desired Sir Antony that a physician should attend her as soon as he had seen the tragic figure lying upon the deathbed. I was in no doubt that a few moments would suffice for it to be obvious that the spark of life was utterly extinct, and the poor wretch lay beyond the care of any physician.

Dr. Langridge from Bridgwater, the town nearest to here, was called, a stable boy riding to fetch him. The doctor is an elderly gentleman and was well fortified with spirits, I fear. When he arrived, I followed him up to the young man's room, intending to offer assistance if it should be required.

He was closeted in the deceased's room for but a few minutes, as I surmised. I was standing at the entrance as he bent over the bed, and I heard him say, "Quite so, quite so—and here is the cause of it!"

It was a bottle of poison. He took out the stopper and sniffed at the little vial. "Ah, the smell, quite typical of prussic acid."

It was a tiny blue bottle, as is usually employed to contain poisons.

"Highly corrosive," said old Langridge. "Death is instantaneous and frightful—mortal poison!"

Then he placed the bottle again on the table beside the bed, from whence he had taken it, and left the room, and I heard him murmuring for a few minutes with Sir Antony in the passageway outside.

"A terrible accident—yes indeed, I can see no other explanation of the circumstances," the old fellow was mumbling. "Yes, these young men can be so unwise, they will take part in some experimentation or other, even when it involves taking risks with their very own lives! I daresay that is exactly what has happened here, Sir Antony; my foolish young colleague was trying out the properties of the drug and took enough prussic acid to put an end to his life! Here is the bottle; it was on the table beside his bed, and you see it is quite empty. What a tragedy . . . Yes, thank you, sir, I'll be obliged for a dram of brandy before I call on your lady. The night is getting chilly, you know, very unwholesome . . ."

They went off into the hall and the door closed behind them, and after a few minutes there came a rather dragging tap at the door and the doctor entered Lady Jesmond's room. Plainly, there was little to be done except to try to calm her nerves, and after seeing that she had some sleeping-draft for the night, Dr. Langridge took himself off, doubtless to snore the rest of the night through till he should arise to compose his bill for attendance.

I slipped downstairs again to Lady Jesmond, who was weeping and exclaiming all the while. I cannot reproduce all her cries and disordered remarks, but I set down the gist of what she said, which was, when I reflected upon it, a strange account indeed of the end of a young man who but a few hours previously had appeared in perfect health—at least, so far as an untrained eye might judge. My lady's talk went something like this, all rushed out exceeding fast, with gasps and sobs intermittent.

"Oh, how dreadful—why, this is the most frightful thing. I heard a noise, you see, a loud banging, almost a sort of drumming—in the room above me, and then a voice calling out, or groaning, rather. Yes, it was more like the groaning of a soul in pain, more of a general sound of suffering, *you know, an agony—so I pulled my old silk wrapper about me and ran upstairs and tapped at Dr. Kelsoe's door, for his room is directly above mine and the noises seemed to emanate from thence, but there was no answer at all, so I opened the door and there I saw him—oh, the poor young man!"*

And so she continued in this vein, and could tell us nothing of what she actually observed when she entered the room, for she was overcome with tears and agitation each time she reached this point in her narrative.

She has, I believe, the kindest of hearts and was weeping half the night. It was sad indeed to see such a carefree and pretty creature cast into such a state of agitation. The housekeeper seemed greatly distressed also by her mistress's unhappiness. She is a good creature who came up and sat beside the bed, until at last my lady fell asleep as the draft took effect, but so late was the night advanced that dawn was fast approaching.

The master of the house has taken charge of events calmly enough—he is such a dry old stick you were as like to find tears coming out of an Egyptian mummy as out of Sir Antony Jesmond—but he seemingly did all that needed to be done straightaway. He has written to Dr. Kelsoe's family to inform them, but I believe they are residents of Lancashire, and Sir Antony's letter is not like to reach them for a week or more. There is no parson near, for Jesmond Place is an isolated house, but the local curate has been informed and in the graveyard here this unlucky young man will no doubt find his last resting-place.

And there, with his quiet grave, the matter should end. But I am much troubled in my mind by some of the circumstances, which Dr. Langridge did not note.

Here I paused in my reading. The day had brightened now. Belos entered the library to light the fire, which was still usual in that cool May. Showers of sparks spurted up and crackled round the logs, hissing as the fire took hold and the rough bark blistered and the resins ran out and caught the flames.

Points of fire reflected on silver candelabra and gilt bindings. Warmth and light made a patchy invasion of this end of the long room: the other seemed now cast into a corresponding darkness, fitfully dispersed by leaping and restless shadows as clouds scudded overhead.

An anxiety was overtaking me: I did not trouble to pull up a chair, but read on, leaning at the side of the hearth, propping my elbow upon the mantel. Elisabeth's writing continued even and steady as ever, her flowing script carried over the pages, yet the matters of which she wrote were deep and puzzling, as she herself commented.

No, there was nothing unusual about the bottle of acid. But what bothered me, and still troubles my thoughts, was that it had been placed neatly upright upon the night-table beside the bed. That, and a circumstance which I did not immedi-

ately apprehend, so entirely natural did the arrangement seem at the time. But I distinctly recollect it, and it troubles me now: I can see old Dr. Langridge standing beside the young man's bed. And then comes what is so strange! I have been over it several times, picturing it in my mind's eye, and I am persuaded that I cannot be mistaken.

Dr. Langridge removes *the stopper from the bottle and sniffs at it, exclaiming at the odor of poison.*

But how came the stopper back into the bottle?

That is the point that I cannot quite get over, although it appears to have passed quite unnoticed by the old physician. Yet how should a man be supposed to toss down a bottle of corrosive poison and replace everything as neatly as if he had taken a sip of cordial?

For there was no sign of disorder. The sheets were drawn up carefully and folded down under the chin of the poor fellow, as neatly as if he had just got into bed for the innocent sleep of a child tucked in by its nurse.

Perhaps, Ambrose, I am too suspicious, as the sad experiences of my earlier life may have tended my mind in that direction; having seen crimes committed, I now suspect them everywhere. But all the circumstances of this young man's death trouble me excessively still. I know little about the medical effects of poisoning by prussic acid, but I have always believed that it provokes the most fearful and instant agony, so that to have time to climb neatly into bed, to stopper the bottle, to fold down the bedclothes as if one were preparing for a night of blissful rest—all these, I believe, would simply not be possible. The agony must surely be so great that the deceased must fling himself about and render his linen into total disorder, and the throes of pain and death would surely descend instantaneously, the moment that he swallowed the dreadful draft.

I think it unlikely to have been Lady Jesmond who put the stopper back into the bottle and tidied the bed-linen—she was in a state of great confusion and hysteria. Nor was it the old doctor himself, for it was all done before he arrived.

And then, Dr. Langridge's suggestion of an experiment . . . What experiment should John Kelsoe have been undertaking in this way? To determine what would be a fatal dose? If so, had he taken any previous quantities, were there any notes made of the measures, any record kept of the dosage? There seemed not to be a single scrap of paper in the room, save one lying near the door, which I stooped down and picked up—yet it appears to have no bearing on the matter of the death. But it was all I could see.

She had enclosed it. A crumpled slip of paper fell from the pages of the letter, and I smoothed it out. It was a yellowish scrap, seemingly part of a list.

Coals of fire.
Quicksilver.
Cakes of glass.

I studied it for a few moments. Odd, that the handwriting was not the quick educated scrawl of a young medical man but uneven and shaky, the black ink spidering across the paper in the way of elderly penmanship.

The meaning, if any beyond some gibberish scribbled down by a doddering old member of the Jesmond household, escaped me. I returned again to the letter.

There is something most extraordinary about this whole matter. It seems we are asked to believe that a medical man, presumably well-informed about the dangers of prussic acid, suddenly swallowed the contents of a bottle of the same, climbed quietly into bed and arranged everything most considerately and carefully around himself. Then he gave some terrible cries and expired!

So had someone in this house entered the room and carried out these small and horrible acts of domesticity—but without raising the alarm or even making any attempt to save the unfortunate young Dr. Kelsoe?

That is what troubles me so, for there is something so precise and so inhumanly cold about such actions. I keep wondering which of my fellow-creatures here at Jesmond Place might have been capable of them.

Poor young man! That is all I can say about Dr. Kelsoe, for I scarcely knew him before his untimely death.

Lady Jesmond's distress has been plain for all to see—or rather to hear, for she cried and wept all the next morning also, while various callers—first Dr. Langridge once again, then the parson about the funeral arrangements—came and went. She has a tender heart, but as you may imagine there are certain uncharitable souls who will think the worst.

There is to be a Coroner's inquest upon the unfortunate young man, but Dr. Langridge has already intimated that he will be strongly inclined to favor accident as the probable reason for this tragic occurrence, and the Coroner is Sir Edward Knellys, who is well-known to Sir Antony.

Ambrose, I would, in my heart of hearts, desire to leave Jesmond Place, but Lady Jesmond, poor affectionate creature, seems to need companionship so much, and I cannot be unfeeling enough to abandon her. Sir Antony we never see all day, not till dinner-time. Mrs. Romey has instructions to take his meals into his chamber upon a tray, and to collect the empty tray when he rings. At other times, the servants are not to disturb him. These are Sir Antony's orders: any disobedience will be punished with dismissal, he says.

Forgive me for my long account. In my distress at the cruel currents that lie beneath the surface of our existence here at Jesmond Place, I can turn only to you. It may well be better that you and I should take our separate paths through life—yet, as we have said in the past, it seems that we cannot live together and we cannot live apart!

I trust I may hear something from you. My compliments to Master Belos.

Elisabeth.

There was something added in an uneven and splashed hand, as if written in great haste just before the letter was sealed.

I beg you to come! E.

CHAPTER 3

AN interruption came before even I, Ambrose Malfine, precipitate though I am, had decided upon a course of action. It is very true that "When sorrows come, they come not as single spies but in battalions."

Belos had entered the room as I reached the end of Elisabeth's communication, with its alarming suspicions still moving through my mind. Before I could say anything, he hurried up.

"My lord, I have heard something that means I must beg leave of absence for a few days."

"Why, Belos, what's the matter?"

"There has been a strolling actor from a troupe going to Bath, who stopped a while in the alehouse, when his horse went lame just the other side of the village. And he brought some news last night . . ."

"News, what news?"

"Tragedy, my lord. True tragedy."

"Good God, man, what's the matter?"

"Kean is dead."

"Kean? The actor, Edmund Kean, d'you mean?"

"Aye, my lord, the greatest Shakespearean of our generation. It is said that watching him act was like reading Shakespeare by flashes of lightning. My lord, his Macbeth was so . . . so *terrifying* that the whole audience jumped if a board so much as creaked in the pauses of his speech. He is to have a great funeral at Richmond, with all the actors from all the London companies in attendance and Macready himself will give an oration."

"And you naturally wish to do honor to the great leader of your profession, although it is so long since you yourself trod the boards. But I suppose an old war-horse still snorts at the sound of the trumpet—pardon me, Belos, that was somewhat clumsily expressed. You naturally, as a former actor, wish to attend this perf . . . —this funeral at Richmond. Well, you had better take yourself off then. Shall we say it might take you the best part of a week to get to Richmond and back? I suppose the day of the funeral is fixed, but I have no doubt it will be a most elaborate occasion that will have taken some time to arrange, so if you leave now you should make Richmond in time."

"Thank you, my lord. I'll get some things together and leave right away."

Belos bowed, perhaps somewhat deeper than might have been necessary.

There was, of course, no doubt that he could have had as much leave from my service as he desired. Ever since he had brought me back from Greece, half-dead from wounds as I was, and nursed me back to health at Malfine, I had from time to time asked him to consider if his interests were best served by remaining buried in the heart of Somerset. He had been on tour with a troupe in Greece when he had met with misfortune and I, enthusiastic young hero as I was then, took him into my service. If I had saved his life, which then looked near to expiring from starvation, a short while later, when I was wounded, he repaid the favor a thousand-fold. He beat off the doctors who would bleed me of the few last drops of red blood I possessed, and got me on board a ship bound for England. It was thanks to him I was now at Malfine, where I had eventually recovered from the Turkish saber-slashes whose scars would never quite disappear.

I would find it difficult to describe Belos, if I were required to set it down. Say that he were missing and I had to give an account of him—why, the truth is that the man is a kind of chameleon, yet nothing very remarkable in any particular. His age, for instance. I conjecture he is somewhere about his fortieth year, but would hesitate to lay any wager upon it. His eye is of a light-brown color, or so I think, yet now, when his face is not before me, I wonder if it is not truly more inclined to lightish gray, for sometimes it seems so in my recollections. But his hair is surely something of a grayish-brown—and yet again, it can look quite dark in certain lights. His height—well, he is of average height, for I tower over him with my lanky shins, yet somehow I do not *feel* as if I am of greater height than he.

All in all, you would say that Belos is a perfectly unexceptional personage, *"l'homme moyen sensuel"* to perfection, of whom no notice would be taken in any crowd or assembly. How could such a man ever dominate a stage, you might think, or move an audience to fright or tears?

And yet there are certain things that mark him out. He has a most deep and mellifluous voice, which somehow leaps forth and carries without the slightest effort to the farthest corner. Belos may stand in the great entrance hall at Malfine announcing a visitor, and as it were *throw* his voice into the air so that it ascends up the great staircase and round the marble hallway. The name of some pot-faced local worthy who desires an interview with the master rings out as sonorously as an iambic pentameter winging its way to the gallery of the Theatre Royal.

This is of course a particularly valuable faculty for a servant in my employ, for it allows of a dramatic delay, a pause which gives me plenty of advance warning to avoid my neighbors, and most especially the damned parson.

However, Belos is extremely reticent about the past and does not usually mention his thespian history, and I was therefore somewhat surprised by his desire to do homage at the funeral of Edmund Kean.

I would have even gone so far as to suspect him of an intrigue, which I myself might well have embarked on under such a cover, *viz,* one so outrageously dramatic that it would probably approach the Venetian carnival in atmosphere. But this gave me occasion to reflect for a moment upon that scene of general carnal intrigue, and I realized that I had never heard Belos express an interest in the warmer passions. He had, it is true, once mentioned a soprano at La Scala with tenderness, yet with a kind of actorish pose that made me suspicious that he had no real entanglement with the lady. Was it possible that he had other inclinations, which might flourish on a foreign soil better than in our right little, tight little island?

But his distress at Kean's death was real enough. And I bade him farewell with a good grace; it suited with my own desire remarkably well, for that desire, as the reader of these pages may have deduced, was the urge to ride immediately in the direction of Jesmond Place and see to the safety of Miss Elisabeth Anstruther.

Yet I would not give in to that desire. I had absolutely no intention of becoming enmeshed in the murderous coils that lay brooding in that household. On the contrary, I laid Elisabeth's letter down on my library table, took up a volume of John Locke, and with my intellect attempted to overwhelm my natural inclinations.

No, I would not indulge her! She had made the decision to leave my roof, she had decided that my protection was not needed—and now at the first sign of anxiety she was begging me to run to her side! Well, let her leave Jesmond Place of her own accord—she was a free creature, not tied to the lady's side with a leash. She could depart at any moment. It was certain that she owed no duties toward Clara Jesmond—why, Elisabeth had scarcely known her for five minutes altogether!

"No, indeed!" I exclaimed, striking the table with my hand. "If she is fearful of the events in that house, let her leave! She can go to her mother's house in Bristol if she will not come to Malfine. *I* am not responsible for her!"

And yet . . . I knew she would not leave the Jesmonds. I knew it with my inmost heart, as I knew hers. For this thing we share, she and I, that we have a perversity, like cats cornered by a pack of hounds, that makes us turn and fight when we should run away. Wherever there is a prudent course in one direction, there will you find us embarking upon another! No, my Elisabeth would remain at Jesmond Place, where some silly woman possessed of a pretty face and an old husband sobbed her heart out over a fool of a young doctor who had somehow contrived to up-end a bottle of prussic acid into his own maw!

I still cannot account for immediately laying down the book, stalking round to the stables, saddling up Zaraband and leading my fine Arab beauty out from her stall, while John Locke slumbered undisturbed upon the library table.

Zaraband's deep bay coat was gleaming like satin in the light spring sun. She was fresh, even frisky, dancing across the cobbles, and her elegant head strained for the gallop. But we had to defer that at present: there was someone near at hand whom I desired to consult.

We therefore took a path, pleasantly overgrown, that led through the grounds of Malfine. It was a brighter day than expected; from time to time birds flew up from the hedgerows with a sudden fluttering, and dog-roses twisted in and out of the tendrils of greenery. I know these pale pink simple flowers to be dog-roses, having been instructed in the matter of roses by the lady of Lute House. I myself prefer lusher blooms, but I grant that on a fine day in early summer these wild English things are well enough.

It was this lady, Mrs. Florence Sandys, who opened the door to me herself as I tethered Zaraband nearby, outside the fretted woodwork of the porch.

"Ah, Lord Ambrose! I am afraid you have just missed my husband."

"I'm sorry to hear that, madam. There is a scientific matter on which I had hoped to consult him."

"Won't you come in and take a dish of tea?"

As I entered the parlor of the house, a room somewhat over-cluttered with ornaments for my taste, Mrs. Sandys added, "Adams, the groom from Westmorland Park, just came to fetch him. You know our neighbor, Lilian Lawrence, the former Miss Westmorland, is expecting an interesting event . . ."

"Ah, madam, I never listen to gossip." I dodged a pie-crust table adorned with a long-eared porcelain rabbit nibbling a bed of bright green china lettuce. She looked suspiciously at me but I did not flicker a muscle.

"Very commendable of you, Lord Ambrose, and of course I myself *never* tittle-tattle. I merely take an interest in my neighbors' well-being."

"Yes, of course, Mrs. Sandys, and most admirable it is, too."

The lady relaxed, and rang for tea as we settled ourselves in her parlor chairs. My damned long legs were forced to fold up like jack-knives.

Florence Sandys, the wife of our local medico, was wearing a light snuff-colored gown with a muslin collar, pretty, but not fashionable. This, in a way, is a relief to me, not to have fashionable neighbors, and the Sandys can be valued for better things than the cut of their coats. Sandys had tended my wounds on my return from Greece, when I was dragged back to Malfine half-dead, with saber slashes on my face and body, a gruesome sight that had aroused much local excitement. And barely had I healed up when I got drawn into a couple more confounded scrapes—one on behalf of that very Mrs. Lawrence whose first *accouchement* the good sawbones was even now attending.

The maid entered with Mrs. Sandys' best Worcester china on a tray. The room was cool and agreeable, and if Mrs. S. was not fashionable, she was possessed of good sense, thought I, watching her pouring out smoky golden liquid.

The Sandys moved here from Edinburgh, where he had trained. There, as I understand, Murdoch Sandys had a flourishing practice and of course many colleagues within call, but as his wife sometimes exclaimed, they were subjected to much dirt and noise, such squalor and wretchedness within the city. So when Murdoch's Aunt Isobel bequeathed Lute House to them, they seized the opportunity to lead the rural life, and transported themselves, bag and baggage, to Somersetshire. "And, Lord Ambrose, although Murdoch may have no colleagues to call upon for consultation in difficult cases, he has no rivals either!" This was what Mrs. Sandys had said to me, when she was one day explaining the reasons for their move.

So here at Lute House behold them now, and Florence Sandys has roses blooming in her garden till late into the year, though Zaraband has a penchant for them and is liable to munch away on her finest damask blossoms. In fact, as I looked through the window on that very occasion I could see a particularly fine Empress Josephine bloom dangling from my horse's long velvet muzzle. Ah well, another apologetic bunch of grapes would have to be dispatched to my hostess from the Malfine vine!

As I raised my pink, green and gold cup to my lips, there was a crunching of gravel outside the window and Murdoch strode in.

"Ah, Lord Ambrose, welcome! What brings you here?"

Mrs. Sandys rang for another cup, and her husband greeted her anxious inquiries about Lilian Lawrence with, "No need for anxiety. A false alarm, my dear. I think we must wait a little longer. Ah, excellent tea. Is there anything to eat?"

Over slices of seed-cake, I acquainted Sandys with the events which Elisabeth had outlined in her letter.

"How very strange!" Sandys sank back in his chair, pulling the cravat from his neck. "The young man dead of corrosive poison and the bottle neatly re-corked and replaced on the night-table! Well, I confess the operation of prussic acid is not a speciality of mine—I have scarcely encountered a death from it in my career, though it is quite easily obtainable. But what you describe seems most unlikely, and very intriguing to a medical man. I shall consult my textbooks. Do you intend to go to Jesmond Place?"

No, of course I did not. I thought there was a glimmer of regret in Sandys' eye, though Mrs. Sandys was plainly relieved. I suppose she did not want her husband chasing off into that somewhat peculiar household.

I had no intention of going after Miss Elisabeth Anstruther.

I therefore cannot account for what came over me when I returned to Malfine.

CHAPTER 4

OUR way lay west and we took the coast road. Zaraband was in fine fettle—there is nothing so lovely as an Arab in full stride, racing like the west wind itself, yet with the smoothness of a fast-sailing ship gliding over a glassy sea. I gave the horse her head, and reckoned that we should reach Jesmond Place by late afternoon.

By now, I had to admit my anxieties and my thoughts served only to entangle them with a damned forest of feeling and desires. I imagined Elisabeth's pale face, her tawny-yellow eyes, the slim movements of her body; I thought of poison, of traps, of death. Why had I not begged her to stay at Malfine?

I knew why and cursed myself for it: the devilish contrariness of my nature and my pride. For these I had risked my dearest creature, the closest thing to my own soul that I could encounter on the face of this earth. Instead of persisting, instead of begging that she stay, rather than plead with her to be my wife and remain at my side, I had let her depart to risks and dangers from which perhaps I could not protect her. In these thoughts, of course, I had forgotten her own determination.

There was an inn on the road which I noted as being probably the nearest habitation to Jesmond Place. The Green Lion had an unusual sign hanging outside, on the corner where a side-road turned off into the village of Combwich. Crudely painted, it showed a prancing beast daubed with a touch of worn pea-green paint. Beyond the inn I could see the main street, probably the only street, of Combwich leading narrowly down, as slumberous as any sight I ever saw. The mud-flats of a tidal creek gleamed silvery-brown on the horizon beyond.

Still on horseback, I called to the landlord, who had emerged in curiosity at the clatter of hooves outside. Behind him, a woman had appeared in the doorway and stood in the shadow.

In English inns, ale or cider is always my preferred drink: better good beer than bad wine, and she brought me out a mug and a flagon. In the sunshine, I saw a handsome, well-built woman, her curly hair still black and glossy. Taking a long pull from the mug, I slid down from Zaraband's back and fell into conversation.

"Excellent cider!"

"Thank you, sir; we have our own apple orchard for it."

"How are the deer thriving this autumn?"

"Aye, fine. Reckon us'll have a good winter. Furze blossom be out late—deer'll be fat come spring."

"Yes, very true." In this exchange I was hopelessly at sea, since for all I know, furze blooms be out till the cows come home, whenever *that* may be, but some rural pleasantries must be endured.

"Has your worship come far?" said the landlord.

"From near Minehead."

I did not want to mention the exact place. Better at this stage to keep my identity quiet than to mention Malfine, which someone might well connect with Miss Anstruther at Jesmond Place, since her residence there would have been well-known to most of the county. If I wished to make some discreet inquiries, then I desired them to remain discreet, and to have no blabbermouths busily dispatching rumors about some sinister rider snooping around after Clara Jesmond's companion.

"You've come to see someone in Cummage?"

Cummage? Ah, the local pronunciation. But why should the landlord step back as he asked the question, as if the possibility disturbed him? As far as I knew, Combwich was a harmless village, as stuffed with stick-in-the-muds as any in rural England, none of whom was likely to welcome an exotic visitor such as myself.

"No. Why d'ye ask?"

"Oh, we don't get many visitors . . . the road leads only to the creek, and you, sir, begging your pardon, you have a look about you . . ."

I knew what he would say: "You have a foreign look about you, you with your dark face and eyes and that wicked long scar down your cheek. You do not look like a respectable red-faced squire who might have some ordinary business here," but his wife spoke hurriedly, as if to turn the conversation politely.

"You'll have had a good gallop, sir. If you're wanting a bite, there's cold beef and chutney within, and some bread cobs. There'll be a fresh catch of fish coming in down at the creek on the next tide."

"D'ye have a stable?"

"Aye, round t'back," said the woman.

"Then the cold beef will do nicely."

"That's a damned fine horse," said her husband, as I led Zaraband across the yard.

"She is indeed."

The stables were clean enough, and the provender acceptable to Zaraband.

Once back inside, I was served with a great blue dish upon which lay slices of pink beef with glossy brown pickle heaped at the side, and a plate of the small white rolls known as cobs, together with a rough pat of country butter. The landlord put down a flagon of cider on the table.

"I'll just have to go down to the cellar and see to the barrels, sir, if you'll excuse me, but my wife will attend you."

He called into the back of the inn: "Naomi! Come and see if the gentleman wants anything! I've got to go down below."

She hurried in, perhaps a trifle lonely here in this small outpost; at any rate, I detected a willingness to converse, which was all to the good. There were lace cuffs on her sleeves, I observed as she stretched out an arm to serve me; her dress was rather more modish than one would expect and her feet were shod in elegant shoes of thin green leather.

"Good beef," I said politely. "Excellent rare meat! Is it local?"

"Aye, sir, leastways from a few mile away. 'Course, 'tis mostly fish or venison in these parts, when 'tis in season; we canna' graze cattle on the moors."

"Did I not hear that there was a herd kept at Jesmond Place?"

"Nay, sir, I don't think that be right—leastways, not for

many a year. Maybe Sir Antony's father kept them, but I've never heard of it."

"Well, no matter, but now I come to think of it, is there not some odd story about Jesmond Place?"

The woman turned swiftly and gazed over her shoulder. Her husband was still downstairs in the cellar; I could hear the rumble of barrels being shifted around in the depths below.

"Jesmond Place, sir, is not somewhere I like to go. Though her ladyship is very kind, I do not care for the house, I may say."

"Oh? Then there is some truth in the rumors I have heard?"

The rumors being entirely of my own invention, I could only trust that the landlady would not ask me to give an immediate account of them, but, like so many gossips, she assumed that I was already familiar with the subjects of her conversation. She came closer and sat down on the bench opposite me, settling herself comfortably to begin the tale, which came out in the slow and pleasing local burr.

"Truth? Well, sir, I see it with my own eyes, not a week since, as it were passing along this road! A dirty black cart and piled high with stuff, and the fellow who was driving it, he didn't look like no decent sort to me. Tattered old cloak and his boots all down at heel. He stopped here to water the horses. Said he had goods to be delivered to Jesmond Place—he was to give 'em to Sir Antony particular, and to nobody else. I can tell 'ee something, sir, too—it come all the way from Bristol, that cart! My man axed the fellow if he wanted aught, and he said no thank 'ee—he was damned if he didn't have to take the road right back to Bristol as soon as the stuff was unloaded!"

There were sounds of footsteps approaching, and Naomi rose and was bustling off into the next room as her husband emerged from the cellar, her voice growing faint as she moved away. But I had heard something interesting, nevertheless. Though what to make of it?

Huge tracts of tussocky grassland loomed ahead as I mounted Zaraband; gray furze and the muted purple-greens of heathers gave the land a lifeless aspect—or so thought I. My taste is for the white and salty landscapes of Greece, burning under skies of azure and peacock-blue, but with custom one may acquire a sort of tolerance for these timid English watercolor landscapes, it is true. On a fine day, with a herd of the famous red deer roaming across it, the gentle bluish and lilac haze of the West Country does afford some pleasure to the eye, as does the view toward the distant slate-blue hills of Wales across the Bristol Channel. Here and there, red cliffs of sandstone loomed out of the earth to break the greens and fawns of the palette. I could almost come to enjoy these views, if I submitted myself too long to this contemplative rural burial.

And I have to admit that Jesmond Place, as we neared it in the setting sun, presented a pretty enough picture of the ancient English mansion, if your preference is inclined to the ramshackle, as mine is not. It was a house of gray timbering, surrounded by centuries-old oaks that lined a long driveway leading up to the lichen-clad entrance.

But by now I was not interested in admiring the view. I could think only of Elisabeth, who was somewhere inside that gloomy old house, where the corpse of a young man lay in a bedroom. The story I had heard at the inn had only served to increase my anxieties. What was the strange cartload of stuff that had rolled past the Green Lion? How did it fit into the preoccupations of the household which Elisabeth's letters had described?

Zaraband galloped at a cracking pace up the drive of Jesmond Place. I flung myself down from the saddle and strode up the steps to the porch, striking rather than merely knocking on the oak timbers of the ancient door at almost the same instant as I thrust it open and burst into the entrance hall.

This was long and dimly lit, narrow, yet with a lofty timbering above that reached up into darkness overhead, and as I stood for a moment to get my bearings a woman ran into the hallway.

"Oh God, we are to be robbed!" she screamed at the sight of me, clutching her necklace.

I put the poor creature's mind at ease. "No, madam, or at least, only of your companion. I beg your pardon for not waiting at the door for an answer. I did not wish to cause you so much alarm, I assure you. I am Ambrose Malfine, and I desire to see Miss Anstruther."

Here I could contain my impatience no longer, and I could not forbear to add, "Immediately, ma'am, if you please."

The woman was gasping with fright, but now she calmed herself, touching her blonde hair with her hand to ensure that the strands had not descended. She wore a gown that I thought was of a rose color, low-cut, perhaps more suited to a festive occasion, but she did not somehow look the kind of woman who would have mourning in her wardrobe. In spite of the fear, there was a sensuality about her.

And anyway, why should she wear black for the death of a young man whom she scarcely knew?

"Lord Ambrose! Oh, of course, we have heard of you . . .

The whole county knows you . . . Dear me, you take us quite by surprise, sir! I am Clara Jesmond—my husband is in his study and is never disturbed by visitors, so I must ask you to excuse him. But I can offer you some refreshments . . ."

As Elisabeth had said, there was a country warmth, a rural grace note, in her voice, which added somehow to her promise of hospitality, yet did not take away the fearfulness which lay in her tones, and which had not entirely abated since she had discovered that I was not some marauder breaking in upon Jesmond Place to snatch her jewels and perhaps cut her throat. There was something curious about this lady, as if she carried some secret thoughts within her, all the time that she was running on with mundane politeness. It was almost—how can I put it?—almost like a parody of a hostess. As if the speaker's mind were elsewhere and the words a speech that had been learned by rote.

"Thank you, ma'am, but I must see Miss Anstruther without delay."

Now I was obliged to admit to myself that I had a feverish anxiety about Elisabeth, which had only mounted as Lady Jesmond spoke, so strangely did this household impress me: a cartload of strange goods delivered here, a nervous hostess. And that terrible death of a young man which had occurred within these old walls, with their softly-decaying timbers, their rot of centuries.

"Why, Miss Anstruther is in the parlor, through there."

Surprised at my request, Lady Jesmond indicated a door on the right of the hallway, and stepped back to allow me to pass. I was across the hall and in the parlor in two strides.

Elisabeth looked up suddenly from a chair at the side of

the fireplace, and the relief that rose up in my heart somehow propelled me across the room and I took her in my arms.

I heard somebody—presumably Lady Jesmond—gasping in the background but, like everything else in our surroundings, it seemed at that moment to be faint and distant.

I was aware of a coughing from somewhere behind me, and a murmured few words, "I'll just see about some—some refreshments!" and the scurry of feet pattering away into the depths of the house.

I did not lose my chance.

"Come back to Malfine! There may be some danger here and I do not want you to run the slightest risk of it!"

"No, I cannot. Not yet, Ambrose. I cannot leave Lady Jesmond—she has no other friend here."

I tried further to persuade Elisabeth, but my lady herself slipped back into the room, followed by a middle-aged woman wearing a plain dark dress, full-skirted and rustling heavily, and with an apron tied round her waist and a stiffly goffered mob-cap. She was heavy-set and her plump, pink face was inexpressive, almost mask-like in its lack of suggestion of any feeling. This was the more noticeable as it seemed so much at odds with the full, round countenance and the still-thick gray curls bunched around it. Nature seemed to have intended her to be a warm-hearted motherly sort of personage, but her face was as smooth and featureless as a well-set junket pudding, as if she had pressed out all expression.

The two women were bearing the tokens of hospitality. The older was carrying a tray laden with tea-things; Lady Jesmond trotted ahead bearing a silver tea-pot and water-jug, having evidently adopted that curious English stratagem of pretending that nothing at all is the least out of the ordinary, not even discovering one's paid companion being passionately embraced. Indeed, I thought I almost caught a glance of complicity and a little sideways smile that indicated Lady Jesmond was not averse to intrigue. Certainly, she seemed disinclined to reproach.

When she spoke, I noticed the West Country roughness had almost vanished from her voice, which was now, after the moment of fear had passed, under control and remarkably clear and deliberate. It reminded me of something, but what that was I could not then recall, for it did not seem to have any importance. Later, I reflected upon it, and should perhaps have seen a certain indication at our first meeting, but so often we overlay our memories with present knowledge, so that we cannot discern the limitations placed upon our understanding by past circumstances.

"Lord Ambrose, you will not refuse to take tea with us, I trust? This is our housekeeper, Mrs. Romey."

It was somewhat unusual to go to the trouble of introducing a servant to a guest. I recalled Elisabeth's story of Sir Antony's insistence on observation of the proper forms and this seemed a departure from them, but one for which I liked Lady Jesmond.

Mrs. Romey nodded her head politely in my direction as Lady Jesmond mentioned her name, and began to set the things out on a small table. Then she left the room, as Clara Jesmond sat down, poured out our tea and busied herself with sugar and so forth. Elisabeth had taken a chair opposite her, and I, seeing that there was little point in protesting, sank into another.

"I will be frank with you and say, Lady Jesmond, that I had hoped Miss Anstruther would return with me to Malfine. She may consider it always as her home and I wish it to serve the purpose of sheltering her whenever she may need it."

Clara gave me a rapid look out of those large blue eyes, and I was aware of a kind of shrewdness that I somehow had not expected. Yes, she was pretty, yes, she was clearly distressed by the events which had occurred—and no, she was not entirely without resources, such as estimating the likelihood of assistance from a stranger who had chanced into this stricken household. She was a more interesting personage than she had at first appeared, this Lady Jesmond. She answered me clearly enough.

"Yes, I was aware that Malfine was Miss Anstruther's home before she came to Jesmond Place, and of course, she is free to return whenever she wishes. But I confess I would be sad indeed to lose her company. I am afraid we are not a very cheerful house at the moment, Lord Ambrose, and my husband is so wrapped up with his work. Miss Anstruther is such a kind companion and it would make Jesmond Place gloomier still if she were to depart. And there is surely no cause for alarm—the death of Dr. Kelsoe was a very sad accident, but dreadful things do happen, Lord Ambrose, and we must try not to be overcome by them."

Then why, thought I, is your hand trembling as you pour my tea? A curious lady, in whom fright and philosophical platitudes thus intermingle!

"I do not think it necessary to leave Jesmond Place," said Elisabeth. "At any rate, not for the present. It is very good of you to wish to take me back to Malfine, but I have engaged myself to be Lady Jesmond's companion and that duty I wish to fulfill."

I turned toward her and my eyes were trying to say, "Do not be so stubborn! Come away now, while you are safe."

But she gave an almost imperceptible shake of the head. I know my Elisabeth, or at least, since one can never truly say that of any human being, not even of oneself, I know one thing about her. She experiences fear, certainly—yet she has that cursed stubbornness that will not give way to it. She had sent for me to come to Jesmond Place because she was alarmed, yet she would not desert her post!

My only course appeared to try and stay near here so that I might be on hand to anticipate any dangers that were brewing in this strange household—gloomy even for one where a promising young life has just come to a singularly meaningless and painful end. My mind was coursing round trying to find some way of prolonging my visit when Lady Jesmond spoke again.

"At any rate, Lord Ambrose, you cannot yourself return to Malfine now. It is getting too dark, and the edge of the moor is treacherous unless you know the way. I am sure my husband will wish you to stay to dinner. It will be a simple affair, but you will be most welcome at our table."

There was something charming in the way she said this; privately I did not think Sir Antony would be in the least enthralled to have me as his dinner guest, with my reputation for uncovering skeletons in cupboards and rattling the bones loudly. But it would afford me an opportunity of investigating this odd *galère,* and of staying close to Elisabeth, this annoyingly independent woman whom I had never been able to forget, even when we parted for long stretches of time. Her low voice, her way of moving, the long length of her body, the scent of her thighs—none of these could I obliterate from my memory, even though I might curse at their recollection, which chained me so.

"Why, Lady Jesmond, that would be most kind."

"Good, it is settled then."

CHAPTER 5

DINNER at Jesmond Place could not be exactly described as cheerful, though that was perhaps natural under the circumstances. We dined in a long, paneled room, with a plaster ceiling that was yellowed and dark from candle-smoke. Portraits of long-dead Jesmonds, mostly painted by country daubers, gazed down upon us.

I never cease to thank fortune that my grandfather, old Hedger, was a rich upstart. My father's family line—at least, that section of it which aspired to any kind of portraiture at all—began with that shrewd old devil, which meant that Malfine is not burdened with acres of muddy canvas celebrating my ancestors. Furthermore, those few paintings which adorn its great rooms are by accomplished artists—the Reynolds portrait of my mother, for instance, which conveys her exotic Greek looks and her natural disordered charm, her dark hair straying down over the muslin upon her shoulders, the warm tones of her flesh glowing through the thin fabric.

But Jesmond Place was as full of ancestor-worship as any palace in Peking. Apart from the lifeless long-nosed Jesmond antecedents hanging upon the walls, the room was full of heavy old furniture, much of it black oak and sadly battered with wear. It made an incongruous background for Clara Jesmond; her temperament would, I guessed, incline naturally to a boisterous gaiety, for although she had changed for dinner into a somber dress of a deep blue, smiles kept breaking out as she seemed at moments to forget the sad circumstances in which the household found itself. Evidently she was recovering well from the fits of weeping which had overtaken her at the young man's death. Her hair was piled high on her head in heavy yellow coils, and smoothly parted over her brow in a nunnish simplicity, at tantalizing odds with the *décolletage* of her gown. This was again low over her bosom which looked to be fine still, plump and white, and we were spared little of its charms as she leaned about the table, first in one direction and then in another.

To Lady Jesmond's bosom we owed the only liveliness apparent at the dining-table. Sir Antony joined us, having evidently been forewarned of my presence by his spouse, for he gave a stiff nod and murmured, "Malfine!" in my general direction, I suppose as a species of greeting. He sat in the old black oak chair at the head of the table, facing my lady, with Elisabeth and I between them on opposite sides. There was an empty seat next to mine, though the place was laid, and Lady Jesmond, noticing it with surprise, was about to raise some inquiry, I think, as the dining-room door opened again.

It turned out that there had been another person beneath the roof of Jesmond Place on the night of Dr. Kelsoe's death—a man of whose presence Elisabeth, as I afterward ascertained, had been quite unaware. He entered the dining room now—a small man, bent forward yet youngish, with a pale serious face. He scuttled to his place like a beetle and, hanging his head, muttered apologies to his hostess, who seemed quite amazed at his appearance, looking to her husband for an explanation.

"My dear, this is Mr. Charnock. Malfine, Miss Anstruther, this is my assistant, Charnock."

Then Sir Antony turned. "Why are you late coming down to dine?" This was said quite fiercely to the newcomer.

"I was immersed in my task, Sir Antony. Madam, I must beg your forgiveness. I was quite absorbed, you see."

He turned apologetically, bowing up and down the table so low he almost toppled from his chair, issuing further squeaks of regret and greeting, but did not engage to give us any further information.

Lady Jesmond was still looking taken aback. "When did this gentleman arrive?" she demanded. Mr. Charnock's entry had apparently upset her composure and she tearfully blotted her eyes with her handkerchief. "I did not even know we had a stranger in the house."

This last seemed rather discourteous, spoken as it was in front of the man himself, but Charnock appeared not to take offense. Perhaps, as a paid attendant, it would not have been in his interest to do so, though he looked up with his narrow face tilted toward her ladyship. I noticed that he had a quick, observant, hazel eye—that of a scholar, I would have said, with the pale face and stooping back that accompanies library study: the characteristic air of shabbiness, too, his black suit of clothes much worn and dusty-looking. Yet Mr. Charnock was little more than a boy. His hair was stringy;

he had big hands which seemed somehow uncomfortable amidst the silver cutlery. He gave a rapid birdlike look along the table from time to time, while striving to appear to attend only to his plate.

"Oh, Mr. Charnock arrived the night before last," replied Sir Antony. "I'm sorry, my dear—I meant to give you warning, and then this dreadful business with young Kelsoe quite drove it out of my mind. The truth is that I wanted someone to set my books and papers in order—Charnock here is to be my assistant. Young Kelsoe might have been useful to me, but this man is more knowledgable. I wished merely to keep disorder at bay! I was thinking entirely of you, my dear, and of Mrs. Romey also. I undertake he will be no trouble to you."

The subject of this exchange murmured his agreement. "No, please be assured, Lady Jesmond—no trouble at all, I assure you."

I confess that it did seem odd to me, and I was uneasy that Sir Antony should have been so far heedless as to introduce a perfect stranger into the household without so much as mentioning it to his wife, let alone consulting her opinion before he acted. But she did not seem greatly perturbed thereby. Perhaps after all she was sufficiently distressed by the sudden decease which had taken place, so that having an unexpected personage at the dinner-table scarcely made an impression. Evidently her husband acted in a somewhat erratic fashion and was accustomed to pleasing himself as to who should come and go at Jesmond Place.

But, even granted Sir Antony's perfect right to bring whomsoever he wished into his ancestral home, and given that Lady Jesmond was unlikely to have taken much interest in the personage appointed to sort out her husband's papers, it did seem peculiar that Charnock should apparently be continuing calmly with his tasks. The Jesmonds might not be formally in mourning for young Kelsoe, but surely mundane matters could have been laid aside for a few more days.

As if to emphasize this point, Lady Jesmond mentioned the subject. "Lord Ambrose, you have perhaps heard that we have had a tragic accident here. The young doctor who was to have assisted my husband . . ."

"Yes, Lady Jesmond, pray do not distress yourself. I have heard of the unhappy event."

The housekeeper, Mrs. Romey, entered at this point. Sir Antony coughed and seemed to feel the need to say something appropriate. "A talented young fellow, Kelsoe. A sad business—still, I have made all suitable arrangements. The funeral will take place tomorrow."

At this, the conversation fell silent. Various dishes were now set on the table, Mrs. Romey going to and fro to fetch them, and we served ourselves, our hostess occasionally pressing us to take some choice tidbit, in the generous country custom. The food was plain, heavy stuff: capons, a roast of mutton, an apple custard, washed down with drafts of a dull Rhenish. I noticed that Elisabeth, whose family were wine importers and kept a fine cellar, sipped cautiously at her glass.

Somehow, though my lady attempted to make one or two sociable remarks, the atmosphere grew duller and duller, till it weighed on our spirits like lead and dampened all Lady Jesmond's efforts to converse.

I wondered where young Kelsoe lay this night, the last before his funeral among strangers, his final night above this earth.

Sir Antony excused himself as soon as he had finished his meat, adding, "The funeral is arranged for noon tomorrow. Malfine, will you attend?"

A human touch appeared to be overtaking Sir Antony, for he concluded, "There will be few enough mourners. It would be a kindness if you would stay." There was no desisting from such a duty, and I murmured my willingness to grace the obsequies. Sir Antony seemed satisfied, nodding his head in my direction, and the little fellow followed him hastily as he left the room.

Lady Jesmond said politely, as if to ignore the sad subject and attempting to make up for her husband's abruptness, "You will stay the night, Lord Ambrose, of course, in any case. You could not possibly leave for Malfine at this hour—and it is very misty outside."

I made the appropriate noises, first demurral, then acceptance, followed by thanks. When dinner had been concluded I briefly visited the stables to assure myself that Zaraband was well-tended, listened to her comments and reproaches, left the soft animal-smelling warmth of the stall and returned to the dark old bulk of the house.

The housekeeper showed me to my room, which featured a great four-poster with a lumpy mattress, but who was I to behave like the princess with the pea? Someone had at any rate lit a fire in the chimneyplace and thoughtfully put a heavy woolen robe to warm in front of it—Mrs. Romey, probably.

Elisabeth's room was easily enough found, from the descriptions of the house she had given in her letters. I do not propose to describe our passion here, save to mention that we had been apart for some time and our desires were correspondingly greater. With any other woman I might say that

I enjoyed the usual pleasures, but there is no woman like Elisabeth, which is why I am always hungry for her as for no other.

It was therefore well into the small hours of the next morning when we became aware of the world beyond the flickering candles of her room, as the sound of galloping hooves awoke us.

From below Elisabeth's window came the gasping of a tired horse that can scarce have needed reining in. There was a jingling of harness, the sound of the animal being led away, presumably to the stables at the rear of the house, and then followed a torrential hammering on the great oak door of the house and a hollering below.

Elisabeth's window was at the front of Jesmond Place, on the same floor as Lady Jesmond's, but on the other side of the staircase from it. Next to my lady's was the chamber of the master of the house.

The principal personages in this drama were therefore all roused by the banging and shouting, and I flung on my robe and slipped quickly out of Elisabeth's room, starting immediately down the stairs, so that, as was my intention, it was taken for granted that I had innocently emerged from the chaste bachelor's bedchamber allotted to me, in order to investigate the clamor.

Sir Antony was up already, clad in his nightshirt with a heavy gown thrown over it, but he seemed unalarmed at the pounding to which his house was still being subjected. Indeed, he seemed quite unsurprised, and hastened down the staircase without hesitation, scarcely acknowledging me as he passed, and scurried along the hall to the entrance. I formed the rapid impression that husband and wife had occupied different beds: my lady was still in her room.

Heigh-ho, if our host and hostess did not enjoy the pleasures of the flesh, then at least they had not hindered their guests, thought I with some satisfaction.

Now I could see the housekeeper, Mrs. Romey, a ribboned nightcap on her head and a wrapper thrown around her person, trotting along and calling out the while, "All right, Master Cyriack, all right, I'm opening the door!"

This was, presumably, the son of the house whom Elisabeth had mentioned to me; he who was pursuing his studies at the University but had returned home because of the tragedy. Clearly, he required no further identification than the furious battering that he was inflicting on the door.

Mrs. Romey was by now struggling to pull back the heavy bolts, but the rapid banging nevertheless continued, so that I formed an unpleasing impression of tremendous impatience, rather than an urgent desire for the comforts of home on the part of the hammerer. The housekeeper wrestled with the bolts for a few more moments and then flung open the door, and there came fair bursting in a young man in riding clothes, much splashed and mud-stained, striding across the threshold in his high-topped boots.

"Cyriack, my boy!" exclaimed Sir Antony, and he clapped his arms about the newcomer, but the young fellow broke free quickly from this embrace, and called out to Mrs. Romey: "Ah, Romey, I'm famished! Here have I ridden from Oxford with scarcely a stop and never a divil of a bite!"

He looked about him, and saw myself, who by now had arrived at the bottom of the stairs and was preparing to reascend so as both to avoid what was clearly a family reunion and if possible to rejoin Elisabeth for some morning pleasures of which I did not wish to be deprived by the untimely arrival of this whipper-snapper.

Sir Antony introduced us. "Lord Ambrose, this is my son, Cyriack, and I will say freely that he is something of a renegade. I confess that my dearest wish is that he would pay more attention to his studies, but there, we cannot always have what we would desire in our children!"

It was a rebuke, yet said with tones of pride and even humor, of a kind I had thought Sir Antony unlikely to possess, and which demonstrated to me that Cyriack must be a prodigal, or at least a favorite. Turning to his son, the fond father then indicated myself.

"Cyriack, this is Lord Ambrose Malfine, of whom you will doubtless have heard."

The young man swept off his hat in a low bow, revealing a longish tumble of sandy curls, and contrived somehow at the same time as uttering greetings in my direction to edge along the hallway, wiping his hand on his britches rather than offering it me.

He was a heavily-built youth, who might have had good features and a lively eye, but these were set in a beefy, fleshy sort of face, pouched already, and I guessed it would yield rapidly to dissipation. Some men there are, bulky country lumber such as this lad, whose frame cannot bear the effects even of one night's carousing; others may spend years in debauchery and emerge as sharp and slender as ever, of which I am the very living proof.

However, back to my tale. Cyriack appeared to recognize that some basic courtesies were required.

"Lord Ambrose, I'm delighted to meet you. Of course, yes, you are well-known . . . I trust, sir, you will forgive me. I've done some damned hard galloping and am in no condition for society . . ."

My reputation, it seemed, discouraged further attentions

from Cyriack. What picture had he formed of me, I wondered? A grim and scarred recluse who had ventured forth a couple of times to bring murderers to justice? And, doubtless, that I was the unsociable hermitical owner of the greatest estate in the West Country—every turnip in three counties knew that.

Whatever it was, my notoriety had apparently made no favorable impression on Cyriack Jesmond. He followed hard on Mrs. Romey's heels. She was murmuring, "Very well, then, Master Cyriack, we can find you some cold ribs and pickles . . . and I think there's a raised pie in the larder."

Dear God! Pie and pickles! My heart sank at the thought of the Jesmond larder. However, Cyriack appeared to find this rustic collation attractive and Sir Antony went with them, gesturing apologetically in my direction, but before the little group left the hallway there was a voice from the top of the stairs.

"What is the disturbance . . . Cyriack, is it you?"

It was Lady Jesmond, clutching a long cashmere shawl around her, with her yellow hair hanging down over her shoulders.

Cyriack looked up at her. She was standing at the banisters, leaning over the staircase, and there was a kind of tumbled sensuality about her, a sleepiness and disorder that inevitably evoked the bedroom; I fancied I even caught a trace of sweet heavy perfume that drifted down through the still air of the house, a suggestion of sweat and scent that conjured up, or promised, events of the night.

The young man stared up, a long stare, and she as fixedly returned his gaze. There was silence for a few moments, which seemed somehow to lengthen.

Finally, Cyriack called out, with an odd formality in one

who seemed so quick to haste from the spot, "Madam, I trust you are well, but I beg you to excuse me just at present."

With that, he vanished down into the depths of the house—I presume in the direction of the kitchens.

Lady Jesmond withdrew into her room, but not before I had glimpsed her face, not distressed now, but seemingly hard and impassive.

An odd household indeed. A shouting, mettlesome son, plainly indulged by his father; a woman exuding sensuality, who appeared not to share her husband's bed. And upon her countenance—not at all the appropriate expression for an affectionate stepmother welcoming the son of the house home, thought I, as I bounded back up the stairs to Elisabeth.

CHAPTER 6

BREAKFAST at Jesmond Place on that May morning, with the fresh sunlight flickering in the trees around the house and urging country pursuits on those within, was taken in different parts of the building by the various participants in the dramatic events that were to follow.

Lady Jesmond remained in her room and later on that morning I observed a tray outside her door, partly covered by a napkin, with crusts and coffee-slops on the fine china. I saw no more of her stepson, Master Cyriack, but heard from time to time an outburst of hearty male laughter coming from the nether regions of the house, from which I conjectured that he was entertaining company, or being entertained, in the kitchens. In a place which was nominally at any rate a house of mourning, this did not seem entirely appropriate, but the young master did not appear to be amenable to convention.

As for Sir Antony, he had retreated to his own room and all I knew of how he broke his matutinal fast was what I learned when Charnock appeared in the dining room, where Elisabeth and I were seated at a country breakfast of sausages, mutton and eggs brought in by Mrs. Romey and left to keep warm over chafing-dishes. With the muttering of apologies which I realized was habitual to him, Charnock piled two plates with food and disappeared up the staircase to the regions above.

Elisabeth and I were therefore free to converse, and as might naturally be supposed I pressed her to return with me immediately to the safety of Malfine. Zaraband could carry us both; there need be no difficulty in quitting Jesmond Place without further ado, and my urgings were spurred on as well by my recollections of the pleasures we had mutually enjoyed during the night that had just passed as by my anxieties for her safety.

Again, I expressed my sense of alarm at the oddities in connection with the death of Sir Antony's former assistant. I asked Elisabeth to describe again the scene she had beheld in Dr. Kelsoe's bedroom, and she repeated the strange circumstance which she had observed: that the cork top was firmly lodged in the poison bottle, which had been placed on the bedside-table. And she was able to add a further detail, which she now recalled: "Yes, in my mind's eye I can see the little blue bottle standing beside the bed, with the stopper in place. And it is standing upright on the table, on the white cloth, so it cannot have been thrown there by mischance or accident, as might happen if the young man had raised it to his lips, drained the poison, and then hurled it from him in his agony."

"And yet I believe prussic acid to be a most corrosive substance!" I exclaimed. "How could such a thing as calmly replacing the stopper have been possible if the poison was self-administered?"

"It is very strange, is it not? The poison must have caused an almost instant torment. His mouth and throat were burned—the old physician remarked upon it," commented Elisabeth.

"The body, I take it, is still lying up in the unfortunate young man's bedchamber, waiting for the funeral this noontide?"

"Yes. A woman from the village came to lay him out yesterday. The report has been made to the Coroner, and they do not wish to delay. That, I suppose, is why young Cyriack has arrived from Oxford."

"I presume he has special leave from his tutor," I commented. "I think the vacation has not yet begun, so he should still be at his studies, except for such an extraordinary circumstance as a death in the household. Though I understand he does not apply himself as much as his father wishes—still, I tend to think that a commendation in youth."

"Oh, Ambrose, I beg you to say nothing of the sort to the young man himself. I pray you, do not encourage him—he is already of a most frivolous disposition, I understand. I have not met him before, of course, for he was away at Oxford when I came here, but I gather from Lady Jesmond that his father despairs of him."

"And what do you think Lady Jesmond herself feels toward this stepson who is barely her younger by a lustrum?"

Elisabeth answered slowly, frowning as she spoke, as if recalling past conversations. "I had scarce remarked upon it, but she speaks always very coldly of Cyriack, which is unusual with her, for she has a warm and tender heart and is normally quite open-hearted in her dealings with others. But, now you come to mention it, she says very little on the subject of Master Cyriack, and always with her head down or turned away. If she can be said to be ever cold or dismissive, she is so toward him."

"Curious, for one would imagine that there might be an affinity between them, on account of their youth alone."

"Well, he is only at home in the vacations, so they do not see much of each other, I suppose."

"Very likely. But Lady Jesmond and her errant stepson apart, I am anxious about your presence in this house. There has been a death with certain features about it which seem inexplicable, and that would suggest that there might be a risk to any member of the household. If Kelsoe did not die by his own hand, if it was another who re-corked the poison bottle and placed it upright on the table, then that hand may yet have more mischief to work."

"But how could someone else have killed him?"

"Yes, that path is full of difficulties. How came he to drink the poison, unless it was offered in some disguised form? No medical man obediently raises a bottle of blue glass to his own lips, a bottle whose very color shrieks poison and which is distinctly labeled as such, and takes a smart swig of sure and instant agony, on the mere urging of another."

"Yet there was no sign of anything else—no glass or cup beside the bed."

"So let us for a moment propose that somehow another person contrived to make the young man take the fatal dose. The immediate result would surely have been that Kelsoe would have cried out, would have been instantly seized with spasms of pain, would have tossed his body about. So why did the other person—who had administered the poison and must have beheld the death-throes—not simply hurl the bottle down, as if it had been thrown from the deceased's own hand in his last agonies? That would have added to the conviction that this was a case of suicide, whereas the stoppering of the bottle and its careful replacement on the table makes us suspect . . ."

"Makes us suspect murder." Elisabeth was pale, but calm, with her usual swift grasp and directness of apprehension.

"Exactly so. And that is what makes me beg you to leave here and come back to Malfine."

"But if I do that, it will mean abandoning Lady Jesmond, and she was in such a state of distress . . . At any rate, Ambrose, let me stay and support her through the funeral ceremonies. I know she is determined to attend the church and no doubt she and Sir Antony will be obliged to give some hospitality to the mourners, though I fear there will not be many. Dr. Kelsoe's parents will in all probability be unable to make the journey from Lancashire, for his father is an invalid and it is very unlikely that his mother will travel on her own. So I expect that Sir Antony and Lady Jesmond will of necessity be chief mourners. No, I will remain here, Ambrose, for the time being, and offer them what support I may. Then I will return with you to Malfine."

This was the best I could draw from her, though I had my suspicions that Lady Jesmond might not be as afflicted by grief as Elisabeth seemed to imagine. But, as if to echo Elisabeth's arguments, Mrs. Romey appeared just then and asked her to attend Lady Jesmond.

"I believe, Miss, she wishes to discuss the arrangements for this afternoon. She has asked me to ensure that we can offer some hospitality to the mourners when they come back from the church and I am setting up a table of cold meats; Sir Antony will be fetching up some sack and brandy from the cellar. Would you be pleased to come to take a look at the larder?"

Elisabeth rose and moved to the door. I thought that Mrs. Romey regarded me with a frosty eye, but I am used to such sidewise squinnying, especially from respectable personages. My scars incur it and my reputation compels it.

I might have simply remained for a day or two at Jesmond Place, oozing that general bonhomous neighborly support in time of distress such as is expected at funerals, and afterward returning with Elisabeth to Malfine. That would have been the end of the Jesmond Place affair, and I daresay several lives would have been the happier. But I could not resist stirring up these stagnant backwaters, poking a meddlesome stick into the duck pond of country life.

The first piece of interfering which I undertook was to go quietly up the staircase, and then, instead of entering my room at the back of the house, to continue up the next flight of dark oak treads to the next floor.

I found this oddly disagreeable.

The stairs at Jesmond Place were very old—I mean, the planks themselves. They creaked, of course, but that was not what gave me the sense of unease: rather that they were uncarpeted and so very worn, and the sides of the treads all dusty. Mrs. Romey was either not a particular housekeeper, or she did not often ascend to these regions, and I experienced a sense of distance from the rest of the household, an eerie fancy of climbing up and out of human ken.

I suffered no particular qualms on account of the body that lay in the upper regions of this old house, for I had seen death in many terrible forms in my fighting days in Greece. Death from thirst, from infection, the slow and agonizing mortality that is the true portion of the hero, as well as the sudden bloody spilling of guts that is called glory on the battlefield. No, dead bodies do not frighten me, nor Elisabeth neither, for it is one of her charms over me that she does not suffer from false sentiment. Some women might have protested against a night of passion such as that which we had just enjoyed, when a dead body lay under the same roof as our deliciously entangled limbs. What twaddle! The delights of life are too short and rare to be sacrificed to hypocrisy, and the awareness of death can only enhance them. They are a kind of victory over mortality.

I found Kelsoe's room without any difficulty, for Elisabeth had told me in her second letter exactly where it was: over that of Lady Jesmond. There were two large attics facing each other at the top of the stairs, and I knew that Kelsoe must have had the room on the right. Upon the door of the other attic was a heavy padlock, new and shiny; new also were the timbers of the door itself, strong and close-fitting, in contrast with the ramshackle black old woodwork elsewhere.

I would have liked to wait till I was sure there was no one about. Yet it must be now that I took a look at him: in a short time the sad corpse would be committed to the worms. The old iron clock downstairs in the hallway had just struck eleven and the funeral would take place at noon.

There was no point in knocking on Kelsoe's door, yet I found myself doing so in a kind of involuntary way, as if it would be disrespectful to the dead to enter the chamber unannounced, although the poor young man who lay within would hear no more in this world.

I therefore rapped on the door.

And got an answer!

So suprised was I that it took me a moment or two before I realized that the voice came from behind me; turning back, I saw the beaky head and narrow shoulders of Murdoch Sandys emerging up the stairwell.

"Good God, Sandys, you gave me the devil's own shiver!"

"Well, my lord, I've just arrived here, and finding no one about and the door open, I came into the hall, and looking up the staircase I was in time to see a pair of boots ascending out of sight. You know how particular you are in the matter of your riding boots—they are recognized through three counties, as is your horse. At any rate, after our conversation yesterday, this matter concerning the Jesmonds has been preying on my mind! I determined to follow you here and see if I could be of any assistance. But why is no one about? What a strange household this is, to be sure!"

"And about to seem stranger still," I answered, "for there lies in this chamber the body of a young man who may be a suicide or a victim of experimentation, yet who managed to exercise great domestic tidiness in the manner of his demise."

By now, we were in the chamber, which was in truth a large attic, with deep-set windows looking out over the grounds and gates of Jesmond Place.

It was a sweet May morning, and all the sadder for the tragic long thing that lay on the bed, neatly covered with a sheet.

Sandys and I moved closer to the bed and he gently pulled the sheet back.

"Aye, poor lad!"

It was perhaps the truest expression of regret that might

be heard over Kelsoe's corpse, so far from his family and friends.

The face was a dark purplish color, almost violet. It looked to be swollen and bloated, yet I fixed my gaze upon it and was able to discern that this had once been a handsome enough young fellow, the features being even and regular. The body was already in its shroud, the jaws bandaged up, and Sandys gently undid the wrapper. He prised the mouth apart.

I opened the casement.

Sandys was lifting the hand that lay beside the corpse. The fingers were contracted in a claw-like fashion. "The nails, yes." They were tinged dark blue.

Sandys put his face close to the body and sniffed.

"He's been dead three days," said I. "The funeral is at noon, and none too soon."

"Yes, there is a particular smell, beyond the commencement of the processes of decay, and the inside of the mouth is engorged with blood as would be consistent with swallowing prussic acid, and the other signs are also present, the color of the face, the tinge of the fingernails. I see no cause to quarrel with the diagnosis of the cause of death."

"What were you sniffing at him for? Anyone could tell you he's beginning to stink."

"Yes, beneath the odor of commencing putrefaction—"

"Y'mean, he's turning rotten."

"Yes, but there is another scent which is still detectable—the smell of bitter almonds."

"Now I come to think of it, Sandys, Elisabeth mentioned something of the sort in a letter." I sniffed like a fox, closer to the bed. An acrid, nutty sort of smell, quite distinctive.

"Is the bottle still here?"

"Don't think so, Sandys. I can't see it."

I looked round the room, walked to a chest of drawers, rummaged. A few shirts of coarse brownish linen, clean, carefully folded. Nothing more. There was little else in the room: a cloak behind the door. There was a small table beside the bed, with a white cloth upon it, its surface innocent and empty. That was where the bottle would have been, as Elisabeth had described it. The bottle from which this young man had taken his final, fatal draft. No sign of it now.

Nor were there any more scraps of paper like the one Elisabeth had picked up. I recalled its words: *Coals of fire, quicksilver, cakes of glass.* A list, a cypher? There seemed no meaning. Coal—well that was commonplace enough, and coal fires would have been burning in this house; it had been a chilly May till now. Quicksilver—that was mercury, surely? Not exactly a common substance, yet not unfamiliar—used for mirrors, for gilding. If I had the ballroom at Malfine restored, the craftsmen would use it there. As for cakes of glass . . . I confess, I was at a loss. My mind ran only on the Venetian chandeliers of Malfine, and I thought of the skills of the glassblowers of Murano, of their ability to conjure threads of glass as fine as lace, and work the substance into frills and piping as if it were sugar icing. Perhaps that was what was meant—some sort of table ornament? A glass cake, hard as ice and glittering forever, designed to grace a dining-table?

Enough of rambling!

"Come on, Sandys, if you've seen enough. There's nothing we can do here. But tell me, man, you agree with Dr. Langridge's view, that it was prussic-acid poisoning?"

"Yes, I do. The stuff is easy enough to purchase. There is

a commonplace proprietary brand, which contains a strong solution of the acid. The symptoms would appear in a few seconds—the eyes fixed and glistening, the pupils dilated, the convulsive breathing, the agonizing pains. I have not seen many cases myself. Perhaps it is rarer in the countryside than in the towns, where Scheele's acid can be purchased at a number of chemists'."

"It is quite ordinary, then?"

"Oh yes. When much diluted it is used as a remedy for stomach complaints—though in my opinion it is a very dangerous one, and liable to misuse. Let me see, what do I recall from the textbooks in my student days? So poisonous is it that the fumes alone can result in unconsciousness and even death. There was the famous case of a medical man who allowed some Scheele's acid to fall upon the dress of a lady who was standing in front of a fire, so that the drops of poison became evaporated with the heat and she immediately collapsed from the mere fumes. She recovered, though. And there was a case of a young man who entered a druggist's shop and attempted to snatch a bottle of prussic acid from the hand of the shop assistant; there was a struggle, during which some acid was spilled on the face of the attacker. He died in about a quarter of an hour without even swallowing any."

"So it's highly dangerous. Do you think there is any possibility that some could have been taken by mistake in this instance?"

"By the unfortunate young fellow lying in this chamber? None, I would think—for a medical man would instantly recognize the odor, which is most characteristic. It is still lingering here, even though he died several days ago. I'd like to perform an autopsy, as a matter of fact, and if I did, you would smell the poison even more strongly—as soon as I made the first incision in all probability."

"The funeral is to take place at noon, thus I believe an autopsy is a pleasure you must forgo, Sandys. No doubt the pallbearers will be here very shortly. But tell me, suppose he swallowed some poison by mistake—put the wrong bottle to his lips and took a draft, say?"

"Well, then he would instantly feel a burning sensation in his mouth and throat and realize the mistake. There *are* certain measures that can be taken, if the dose has been small. If I remember correctly, pouring cold water upon the spine and administering brandy or ammonia have on occasion saved lives, but only where a very little has been swallowed, or some fumes breathed in. So if he had swallowed a small amount in error, he might try to call for help. But prussic acid produces muscular failure and loss of consciousness much more quickly than any other poison. The jaws clench, the fingers contract . . . there would in all probability be no time to summon any assistance."

"And yet if this young man is supposed to have swallowed the best part of a bottle of prussic acid and then to have carefully replaced the stopper in the bottle and placed it upright on his bedside table, what would you say?"

"Why, I would maintain that such a thing would be quite impossible! The acid would take effect within a few seconds."

"Yet that was what was found here."

"In that case . . ."

"Yes?"

Sandys spoke carefully and cautiously, as he usually did, yet his words had the more effect.

"Some other hand replaced the stopper."

We stared at each other without speaking. For the moment, there seemed nothing more to be said.

As Sandys and I descended the stairs to the first floor, it was clear that there was no need for caution on our parts if we wished to be unnoticed. The devil himself would not have been noticed at that moment, not if he had suddenly materialized on the stairs of Jesmond Place in a blazing halo of sulfurous flames.

"Open the door, madam! I say you shall open it this instant!"

Cyriack Jesmond was pounding in a fury on a door and a woman's voice cried out from within.

"Cyriack, you are behaving like a crazy fellow. Leave off! You have no right to treat me like this!"

"And have I no right, madam? And whose house is this, pray? My father's—and it will be mine one day. And then I'll treat you how I please, you damned witch and whore. You know what they say about you in Combwich!"

As he spoke, he again set his shoulder to the door, which this time burst open, and I could see the terrified face of Lady Jesmond in the room beyond. Cyriack had his arm raised over her head, and his face was contorted with rage, as his anger became fouler.

He thrust his face closer to hers.

"I saw the smoke from the chimney, madam, as I drew near the house. No smoke without fire, they say. I'll have Knellys to you, damn me if I don't!"

Most of this speech was quite incomprehensible to outsiders such as Elisabeth and myself; I am bound to say that intelligibility appeared rarely to have been one of Cyriack Jesmond's prime concerns in any case. But before we could even try to make something of his curious outpourings, Lady Jesmond herself replied.

"Pray, curb your anger, Cyriack, on this occasion at least. Remember there's a young man lying dead upstairs!"

But nothing, not even this rebuke, could stop his anger. His fist clenched viciously in mid-air and she seemed frozen before him like a rabbit in front of a stoat.

He was about to bring his hand smashing down into her face when I managed, with a leap from midway up the flight of stairs, somehow to seize his arm and drag it backward, wrenching it down as we tumbled together and rolled to the head of the next flight.

Cyriack's bellow of rage changed suddenly. I was gratified to hear it become a scream as I twisted his arm out of the shoulder-joint, and heard the scraping of the ball against the socket. I did not release the arm. An agonizing hold: pure hell-fire burning along the nerve. I congratulated myself on still having the trick of it.

"Get up!" The voice came from above us.

Sir Antony was standing outside his wife's room, wearing an old dressing-gown. He looked feeble, but there was some authority still in his face. He looked from his wife to his son.

"Cyriack, I will not endure this behavior! Not even if you are my son—it is intolerable. D'you hear me, sir?"

Cyriack was standing up, nursing his arm.

"Clara has been intriguing against me! And this damned fellow here . . ." He jerked his head in my direction, his lower lip jutting spitefully out.

His father sighed aloud.

Cyriack's excuses died away, as if in anticipation.

"I saw what happened," said Sir Antony. "Tell me no

more lies, my son." Turning to me, he said, "Lord Ambrose, I trust you are not injured?"

"No, Sir Antony," said I. "A trifle dusty from rolling about on your floor—you might tell your servants to keep better vigilance about their work!"

It was a charming family group, which soon broke up. The son of the house flung past me and clattered down the stairs and out through the front door, Sir Antony calling after him: "And we expect your attendance here at midday, sir."

There was no answer but the bang of the front door.

Lady Jesmond, wrapped in a loose overgown, reappeared on the landing, surveying the splintered lock of her bedroom as if she were in a state of staring disbelief and terror.

"I'll send a man to get it repaired," said Sir Antony.

"Lord Ambrose, if it had not been for you, that lunatic would have struck me such a blow as might—"

"Go back into your room and get dressed, Clara."

But before she retreated, Mrs. Romey and Elisabeth appeared from the nether regions of the house, staring up at the tableau. Then the housekeeper rushed up the stairs and, putting her arms round Lady Jesmond, making clucking and soothing sounds the while, she led her into the room beyond. At the same time, Sir Antony also dived back into his own rooms, and the Malfine party, Sandys, Elisabeth and myself, were left staring at one another from our various vantage points.

I thought I saw a thin and stooping shadow move against the banisters on the landing above, outside the room where Kelsoe's body lay.

CHAPTER 7

IT was a sad little ceremony at the church of St. Chad, for so the old and crumbling pile that stands on the edge of the Jesmond estate is called. It looks out toward the hills: I fancy it is even older than Norman, with a low, squat gray tower, much ivied about.

There were more mourners than I had expected, although Kelsoe's own relations had been unable to make the journey from their home in the north. We consisted of the entire party from Jesmond Place, family and visitors, enlarged by the landlord of the Green Lion and his wife, presumably as representatives of the nearest village to the Jesmond estate, with a snuffling young woman in attendance whom I supposed to be their daughter, for she bore a striking facial resemblance to Naomi, the landlady. They had driven over for the occasion in a pony and trap, with a black crêpe bow on the pony's harness, which seemed out of proportion to any grief they could feel for a young man who must have been almost a complete stranger. The chief motive for their presence was perhaps supplied by the eagerness with which the landlady peeped about her, taking particular note of the Jesmonds as they filed past to the family pew at the front of the church.

The church was cold, even on a late spring day with the butterflies flickering about outside, for a chill struck up from the uneven stones of the floor, which were gloomily inscribed with worn and forgotten remembrances to the dead. A few staring white sculptured faces of marble and plaster Jesmonds peered out at us from carved biers set into the walls.

The coffin was carried by six lads, hired from the village, who looked to be wearing borrowed clothes and to have had their ruddy faces compulsorily scrubbed for the occasion. There was not far to go from Jesmond Place to St. Chad's; once inside the church, they set their load down before the altar.

A raw-faced young curate began to drone.

"Who is he?" I muttered to Sandys.

"A curate from a place called Otterhampton," he whispered back. "It seems there is no church or clergyman at Combwich."

"Well, that's something to be said for the place. I suppose Otterhampton is some tiny out-of-the-way speck on the map."

The curate was gabbling on.

"It is somewhat forsaken, I believe. I understand a previous rector kept his horses in the churchyard—and the present one is not much in attendance. But I have been told it is a charming little spot."

I was about to give my views on charming spots, and the unyielding tedium they impose upon their inhabitants, but our conversation was beginning to disturb some of the congregation; the landlady of the Green Lion was peering at us cautiously, turning a fraction in our direction. She had, I noted, as she saw me observing her and turned hastily back, a very fine profile.

The congregation included Cyriack Jesmond—which surprised me, for I had not thought the young man would subdue his temper sufficiently to attend the funeral rites of someone who cannot have been much to him; however, he appeared to have calmed down, so that he stood and sat, and even knelt from time to time, in the family pew, as decency required. Had he even met young Kelsoe? I asked myself. It was quite possible that they had never encountered each other, if Cyriack had been in Oxford for the entire short time that Kelsoe had resided at Jesmond Place. Yet the rebellious son looked subdued—thoughtful, even—as we stood at the graveside after the service in the church was over and all that remained was the sad business of committing the body to the earth.

Lady Jesmond and the other women had not accompanied us to that sad black trench in the green churchyard: she retreated to the house, supported by Mrs. Romey. The mistress of the house wore a broad, shadowy, feathered black hat covering her fair hair and a thick black veil over her face, and I could discern little of her reactions at the funeral service, but directly afterward, as we filed into the hall at Jesmond Place, she threw back the cobwebby netted layers of her veil and I saw her eyes were reddened, the lids swollen.

She had been weeping, but was it for the young man who now lay in the coffin? Or was it perhaps for herself, married to a crabbed old creature with a vile-tempered son? I wondered what would happen when Sir Antony died. By the laws of nature, Clara Jesmond would survive him by many years, and she could hardly look forward to sharing the house with her brutal and foul-tempered stepson.

By now, we had all assembled in the hall of the great house, which seemed older and gloomier than ever. How many occasions like this had it seen? How many deaths? Age is not always a desirable quality, neither in men nor in houses.

The conventional baked meats, joints of beef, a ham and so forth, were set out on a long table, in the old country manner. The village boys, their boots banging on the flagged floor, piled their plates high, bolted down the food and soon departed, Sir Antony pressing coins into their hands as they left. The landlord and his wife looked about them with unabashed curiosity, but ate as heartily as the lads, though the wife and daughter sipped sherry with some gentility. However, they too went off in good time, having stared about them sufficiently, I suppose, and I heard the clatter of their pony and cart departing with some speed. The curate stayed only long enough to make some conventional phrases of commiseration and to collect his fee from Sir Antony.

Charnock, who had remained a slight figure in the background all through the proceedings, was soon accounted for. He had, as he confessed, known nothing of the departed and, stopping only to claim that he suffered from a headache, ascended into the upper regions of the house.

That left the core, as one might say, of the family, if one included Mrs. Romey, plus the Malfine trio. And if there had been a family truce for the duration of the formalities, it was no longer being observed.

Cyriack was not sipping sherry, nor even ale, I observed.

He had poured out a tumbler of brandy and tipped it down his throat, and then turned to pour another from the decanter on the table, his father remonstrating with him. "Damn it, let me be!" shouted the son, then turned to Lady Jesmond and jerked an elbow angrily in her direction. "I suppose you think you'll do for me!"

There was a shocked silence. An uncomprehending one? Yes, I thought so, on the part of Sir Antony, at any rate, who stood beside his spouse as the unruly scion bellowed forth, his voice ringing to the rafters. After all, if anyone was done for, it was the poor fellow whose remains lay even now close by in the churchyard.

Lady Jesmond's face was transfixed, staring at her stepson.

Cyriack went on: "Oh yes, madam, I know you for what you are! The tragedy is, my father cannot see it. But there's no fool like an old fool, you know. None knows better than I!"

Sir Antony broke in at this. "Cyriack, I will not tolerate any more of this! You will return as soon as possible to your studies, and if I have bad reports of you, sir, you may be sure I shall not be generous with your allowance!"

"Don't trouble yourself, Father!" flung back the young man. "Faugh, I need some fresh air! I'm going out for a ride—I've been preached at enough for one day."

He strode for the door, pausing as he did so and half-turning back to the table. "Damn it, I want another drink!"

"No, you've had enough. Cool your head for once, I beg you, sir!"

"Where's my flask? I'll take that—I'll not be back here in a hurry, you can be sure of that. Romey? Romey! Fetch my flask. I'll take some more meat, too—or would you deny me even that, Father?"

I must admit these rural family dramas do add a little

spice to country life. The circumstances here seemed a trifle extreme, but funerals always bring out the worst.

Cyriack returned to the table and hacked off some slices of beef, cramming them into his pockets like a mad fellow, not ceasing in his angry complaints. "At least I'll take what I can eat—you did as much for those village tykes just now! It seems to me there'll be little enough left of my inheritance by the time—"

He was interrupted at last. The housekeeper had slipped past him, up the stairs, and returned with a silver hip-flask, which she filled with brandy from a decanter on the sideboard. She held it out to him and he snatched it from her hand and tore out of the room.

There was a long silence. Sir Antony lowered himself into a chair beside the empty fireplace.

"My God, Malfine, there is nothing like an ungrateful child! 'Sharper than a serpent's tooth'!"

"I think, sir, we should be leaving you."

This was Sandys.

I joined my voice to his.

"Yes, this is clearly no occasion for strangers, Sir Antony."

Only Elisabeth looked reluctant, glancing sadly at Lady Jesmond, who had produced a small black handkerchief and was dabbing at her eyes with it, holding onto the back of a chair the while.

"Yes, Miss Anstruther," she murmured, "I fear you will not wish to remain here now. I had hopes of some companionship, but I see it is not to be! I am sure you will wish to leave with Lord Ambrose and Dr. Sandys—pray do not feel concerned on my account. Your things may be packed straight away—Mrs. Romey will help you. You need think no more of Clara Jesmond!"

Yes, madam, thought I, and I will call your bluff, for I am determined that Elisabeth shall remain no longer in the bosom of such a family.

I do not know whether I would have persuaded her to depart and leave Clara Jesmond to the mercy of her violent stepson, and, to tell the truth, I would myself have had misgivings. But the fact of the matter is that a sudden and terrible event occurred, so that I did not get the opportunity to put to the test my influence over the determined character of Miss Elisabeth Anstruther.

CHAPTER 8

THE little party standing around the remains of funeral baked meats heard Cyriack's footsteps pounding out and down the steps of the house, and then his voice, screaming for a groom to fetch his horse. I was of a mind to go and knock him off the poor beast's back, for he was no more fit to be trusted with a horse than with a woman; involuntarily I followed him to the door and out on to the top of the flight of steps leading up to the entrance. I was in time to see him snatching up a riding-whip that lay on a hall table.

Meanwhile, the party remaining in the great hall, Sir Antony and Lady Jesmond, Elisabeth and Dr. Sandys, moved as if all drawn together by some sixth sense, to the mullioned window which opened on to the front of the house. From my vantage point at the top of the steps I could see their faces through the dim old panes of glass, and, so frightful were the events that followed that the scene is impressed upon my inner eye, and I fancy I can see them yet, standing at the window looking out onto the grounds like a ghostly audience peering into an arena.

Thus it was that we were all spectators of what happened next, watching, with the sensation of people in a trance, as if in apprehension of a drama about to take place before our eyes.

It began almost immediately. A groom came running round the side of the house with a ready-saddled horse, as if he knew his master's demands well enough to anticipate them, and as he halted the animal before the steps, Cyriack flung himself astride it, gave the horse a cruel cut of the whip and aimed another slash at the wretched groom, who leaped out of the path of the prancing hooves as the creature surged forward.

The drive at Jesmond Place is a long one, curving to the entrance, and we could all see what happened next. There was a flash of silver as Cyriack impatiently pulled out the hip-flask which Mrs. Romey had handed to him, screwed off the top and held it to his lips. Horse and rider thundered toward the iron gates, which stood open, but there was a momentary check as they reached them, for they were not fully open and the horse must slow down for a moment to pass through.

What happened next has diverse accounts, according to the eyesight and perception of the spectator concerned, but Elisabeth, Sandys and I agree on the principal points. The horse resumed its headlong gallop, and as it passed through the gateway the rider appeared to suddenly stand right up in the stirrups and to arch backward in a terrible contortion, almost like an acrobat in a circus, which absurd comparison flashed momentarily through my brain as it endeavored to make sense of the scene.

But then all frivolous comparisons were over.

Standing in the open doorway, I heard a most frightful scream, a deep-throated shriek of agony, coming from the direction of horse and rider.

I saw in the distance that Cyriack Jesmond slumped down, seemed to topple forward for a moment over the horse's neck, and then rolled sideways and fell from the animal's back altogether, yet was trapped by one foot which remained fast in the stirrup.

Opposite the gate of Jesmond Place a clump of trees shaded the roadway; the horse now bolted straight out of the gates and between the tree-trunks, its rider dragging behind, flopping horribly upon the rough ground like a gaffed fish. The groom had started down the drive after them, and I broke free of the moment of horror which had frozen me where I stood and raced after him, catching him up with my long-limbed stride, and tearing through the gateway and into the trees, where the horse had slowed somewhat, though I still heard horrid dull sounds as the head and body of its master battered against tree-trunks and crashed through undergrowth.

Running behind it, I called out to the animal with a special whistling sound that the Romanies use to calm a frightened pony. The panting groom was close behind me now and was endeavoring to use up his scant remains of breath by yelling at the horse, but I clapped my hand across his mouth; the animal would not be steadied by further noise and alarums.

Gradually, the terrified creature slowed, and finally stopped. A trail of destruction lay behind it, a bloodied track where young Cyriack had been swept along. Reaching the animal's head, I caught the reins and handed them to the groom with an injunction to make no more of his row. The mouth of the trembling horse was dripping with foam that frothed over the bit and the bridle, and upon the recumbent body of its master.

His face was a mask of blood, mud and saliva, yet, as I bent over the form of Cyriack Jesmond, I realized that not all the slaver around his mouth was splashed from his horse. I tore off my cravat and began to wipe the muck from his face, to try to discern the extent of his injuries, and saw that a glistening foam was emanating from his own lips, which were a frightful purplish-blue in color.

A few words seemed to issue from the contorted lips. I was close to them now. He seemed for a moment to know me. His words were forced out in agony, yet there was a hissing clarity to them.

"The sparks, Malfine! Fire! The smoke at night."

He was still living at that moment, but as I bent over him his jaws clenched together in a terrible grimace and his breath came in long convulsive gasps.

"Make way—let me look at him."

Sandys had reached us now, and was bending over my shoulder. I rose and allowed him to kneel on the spot where I had been, and we watched as the contortions of the body worsened, with a few great jerks of the spine, and the hands cramping tight into claws. The breath was now a sobbing panting, the whole face a horrid bluish color with a cold sweat broken out all over the features. Sandys endeavored to pull back the head so as to allow some air to reach the gasping lungs, but as he did so, there was one terrible final gulp and then no more.

The eyes stared up, fixed, glistening, the pupils huge. The orbs seemed almost to be starting from the head. A peculiar scent arose, not merely the nasty smells of violent death where the body bursts through its sphincters, but a bitter, sharp, acrid odor.

Sandys stood up, brushing leaves and grass from his breeches.

"Poison."

That was the one word he uttered. There was no need, at that moment, for anything more.

CHAPTER 9

THE body of Cyriack Jesmond lay upon his bed; his eighteen brief years in this world were over. There is no purpose in mincing my words for I cannot consider him as anything but a vicious young scoundrel; sooner or later, he would in all probability have been taken out of this life and dispatched into the next after picking a quarrel with some under-estimated and unconsidered personage, yet I could not but regret that he had been allowed to grow into such a young fool and given no opportunity to learn better.

Still, moral reflections bore me, and I did not continue with them. There is an age of creeping propriety descending upon us, and I will resist it with all my powers.

While, therefore, the Jesmond Place household was engaged in the lamentations and exclamations which might be imagined upon the discovery of the son and heir taken so sudden by a dose of poison that he tumbled clean off his horse and was brought back stone dead to the ancestral home, I made it my business to indulge in a little activity.

After Sandys, standing over the convulsed and disordered body in that little coppice of trees where Cyriack's horse had finally been brought to the end of its tumultuous dash, had pronounced life extinct, the groom had run back to the house and fetched a couple of sturdy stable-hands, with a trestle upon which the body of their young master was laid. Sandys, stripping off his coat and placing it over the dead contorted face, advanced before them in order to break the news to the family, but it seemed that they had seen part of the proceedings from the window, for Sir Antony and Lady Jesmond were standing fearfully in the doorway. Sandys strode some yards ahead of the makeshift bier and urged them inside. From a distance, I could see him urgently speaking in Sir Antony's ear as they entered under the old carved stone doorway, as generations of Jesmonds had done before, and I heard a woman's shriek from within the house, issuing through the casement window.

For myself, I did not hasten back. I waited for a few moments, calming the terrified horse that had dragged its master's recumbent form through the trees. I noticed the savage cuts of the whip upon its flanks: one creature, presumably, that would not mourn the passing of Cyriack Jesmond.

I loosened the girth of the saddle to aid its breathing, and as the breath slowed and steadied, took the bridle and began to lead the animal back to the house. The path that we followed was clearly marked with a trail of broken branches and torn shrubbery. The early summer flowers that had sprung up lately were gleaming dabbles of color, and brighter still were the splatters of blood that had sprayed out as the defenseless head of Cyriack had swung against tree-trunks and occasional rocky outcrops. Slowly, we plodded back, returning to the gateway to the grounds of Jesmond Place, and here, just inside the gate, I caught a glimpse of silver among the clumps of green.

It was the dead man's hip-flask, which had tumbled from his grasp. I sniffed at it: a strong odor of spirits, something like a fruity brandy. And something less familiar: that same bitter tang that I had caught on Cyriack's dying breath.

The same smell that had haunted the body of that other young man, just gone to his last resting-place.

I took Cyriack's horse round to the stables and gave the groom some instructions for its care, telling him the creature needed peace and quiet and a blanket over its back. Zaraband gave an anxious whinny as I stopped to pay her my respects. She longed for her daily gallop, I knew.

"Soon, soon," I murmured, but I had to turn my footsteps toward the house.

There I encountered a scene of shock and mourning, which I imagined repeated, yet with even more intensity of feeling, that which had taken place here a few days before. On that occasion, the young man had been almost a stranger, of whose inner life these persons could have known very little; this was the only son of the Jesmond blood, the young buck whom they must presumably have believed would one day inherit all—house, grounds, horses . . . everything; the youth who had grown up within these walls and had played here as a child.

Sir Antony suddenly looked to be an old, old man. You would not have believed that he and Lady Jesmond were man and wife, so ancient did he seem beside her. He had collapsed into a huge chair that stood inside the great hall, and Mrs. Romey was putting a rug around him, for he was shaking as if it were mid-winter. Lady Jesmond was rubbing his hands between her own: old gnarled brown branches, they looked like, between her plump pink fingers. Behind the shadows at the high back of the chair stood Charnock, his face anxious, his own hands twisting together as he contemplated the master and mistress of the house.

Elisabeth entered the room. "Dr. Sandys has taken . . . has gone upstairs," she murmured, and I understood that Sandys had escorted the body of Cyriack to his room.

"Elisabeth, I must speak to you."

I drew her out of the room.

"It was another case of poisoning—I have Sandys' word for it, and I myself saw the signs. I am sure it was the same poison which dispatched young Kelsoe. There is real danger here, believe me!"

To my relief, she answered that I was in the right of it. "Yes, Ambrose, I saw that something terrible had happened when the young man fell from his horse, and when I saw you going after them, I was frightened for you, also."

"Let us all return to Malfine now," I urged, "you, Sandys and I. Sandys' horse is in the stable and Zaraband can carry the two of us. Lose no time—don't stay to be packing. Fetch your cloak and we'll get away from Jesmond Place this instant!"

She faltered. "But . . . Lady Jesmond . . . Can we leave her here? I fear for her, Ambrose."

I was about to say that in my opinion the biggest threat to Lady Jesmond's happiness, her foul-tempered lout of a stepson, had been disposed of, but thought better of it.

"Come with me now and in a few days I will return to see that she is safe—there is an inquiry which I particularly wish to make—and then I will look after her ladyship, trust me in that."

"But supposing the danger is here and now—in this house, *this very minute?*"

It was going to be difficult to persuade Elisabeth to make good our escape, that I could see, but help arrived from an unexpected quarter. Murdoch Sandys was descending the stairs as we spoke, and immediately urged our return to Malfine. When he heard of Elisabeth's fears for Clara Jesmond's safety, he offered a solution to her difficulties.

"I will stay here, Miss Anstruther, at least until the young man's funeral, and take care of Lady Jesmond. You may rely on me as a medical man not to be deceived into danger. I will take every precaution, be assured."

"Sandys, will you have my pistol?"

"No, Malfine, there'll be no need of that."

"Very well." But I, certainly, did not expect to have any need for it where I was planning to go, unless it be to fire a few shots to wake the place up.

"Be so good as to deliver a line to my wife at Lute House," said he.

"I'll fetch you pen, ink and paper," said Elisabeth eagerly. "I have some in my room."

A thought struck me, prompted by Elisabeth's words.

"Now there's an odd thing! In young Kelsoe's quarters up in the attic there was neither pen nor paper to be seen. Yet you would think that as a medical man he would have been in the habit of making some notes, would you not?"

"Yes," answered Sandys, "and besides, did he not have a family in the north of England? Surely he would have wished to write to them from time to time?"

"Yes, and they would write to him!" cried Elisabeth. "His mother—or a sister, perhaps. Surely there would be some correspondence."

"Perhaps he had been here for too short a time for any letters to arrive," said I, though I did not in my heart believe that this was the explanation.

"I believe I heard from a medical acquaintance that he was in Bristol for some months before he came here," was the doctor's comment. "He must have received some letters while he was there—but perhaps he destroyed them all when he came here."

"That would be an odd thing to do. Yet I am sure there was no letter at all in his room," said I.

Sandys spoke slowly, his face grave, as he thought of something further.

"And if it were truly suicide, I heard of no note . . . nothing left to give any of us a reason for the poor wretch's dispatching himself out of the world."

"Well, that may be an argument that it was indeed an accident."

I always approve the clarity of Elisabeth's thinking. "And maybe," she added, "if he desired to write a letter, he borrowed pen and paper from Sir Antony. That would be normal and natural."

Quite. Yet the probability of Kelsoe's death being normal and natural, a mere accident, it seemed to me, was greatly reduced by the terrible eventuality that had befallen young Cyriack. Two young men, two chance cases of poisoning from prussic acid . . . well, that was too much to believe. But I did not voice this thought.

CHAPTER 10

WE rode through that warm night in late May, leaving the dark outline of Jesmond Place behind us, its chimneys twisting above the higgledy rooftop like contorted branches, dark against the lighter summer night. Zaraband carried us both with ease, and so warm was it that I found my cloak to be an encumbrance. At the edge of Exmoor, I stopped, dismounted and rolled it up, intending to strap it on the saddle, and as I did so something rolled out of it. I had feared that if she recognized it, Elisabeth might find it a disagreeable sight, reminding her of a scene which was perhaps better forgotten. But I could not have prevented her seeing it, for it gleamed in the moonlight as it tumbled away. I reached down and retrieved it.

"Oh Ambrose, what is it?"

I tried to make light of the matter.

"I have been stealing the Jesmond silver—that is all."

"It is a flask, surely . . ."

She knew what it was. The flask from which that

wretched young man, Cyriack Jesmond, had drawn his last draft, the final object that had touched his lips before death itself.

"Is there poison left in it?"

She gave a shudder as I thrust the thing into my cloak.

"Only the dregs. But I'll be damned careful not to let Belos get it into the silver pantry at Malfine, I assure you!"

That was all that was said at the time, and we rode on, until the familiar graceful shape of Malfine, the great sweep of the house, its white columns and pediments, was glimpsed through the trees in a soft dawn of tender green and blue. We cantered past the gleaming gray stretch of the lake, startling deer who had come to drink in the early hours of the morning. A white heron, motionless as a statue, stood upon the small island in the lake, where I used to splash and swim as a boy.

While Elisabeth climbed the flight of steps to the great classical entrance porch, I took Zaraband around to the stables. The groom, Pellers, appeared in the stable-yard and, entrusting Zaraband to his hands, I strode again into my inheritance.

There was a frantic barking as I entered Malfine, and then a rushing and flurry of paws and feathery fur which finally disentangled itself into the shapes of two separate animals, each bounding eagerly on either side of me as I crossed the great Italian marble entrance-hall, a vast black-and-white checker-board, on which their claws scraped and pattered. Their collars were of gilded Moorish leather, as outlandish as their names, for Queen Nubia and King Taharka were Salukis, an unrefusable gift from that Nubian potentate whose daughter Sandys and I had contrived to rescue upon a time. Salukis are Arab hounds, fast as the desert winds: some say they were the hunting-dogs of the Pharaohs. They were used in the Arab kingdoms of Spain, in that green terrain of the Guadalquivir where the nobles of Córdoba rode for their sport alongside a river as bright as a scimitar, accompanied by dogs with ears curled like the clusters of hyacinths and eyes as clear as dew.

But, to be more prosaic, if you will consider a sort of golden-plumed greyhound, you have the type of the beast. You may consider, also, the apoplectic astonishment with which they are greeted in the English countryside. "By God, sir, what's that? That's no Jack Russell!" said Squire Anderton, whose lands march with mine, as Nubia came lazily bounding after him one day. "Damn ye, you can't ride to hounds with that!"

No, and you can't outrun them neither, as Anderton discovered a few minutes later when the freakish beast suddenly turned into a streak of honey-colored lightning and sank her long ivory teeth in his britches.

Heigh-ho, what sport! "Tally-ho, sir!" cried I.

But these joyous memories are setting my narrative aside.

A day or so later, returning from an early-morning ride, I led Zaraband back to her stall, and observed that old Dobbie, or as Belos preferred to call him, Barbary, was in his accustomed stall. Belos, then, must have returned from Richmond. No doubt he would be full of actorish doings—even, perhaps, actorish longings. I doubted whether he could in reality long remain contented with playing the part of my manservant. The impulse that had prompted him to join a troupe of players, and then to accompany them to Greece in an ill-omened adventure—that impulse could not have been entirely destroyed by the stifling and lonely life he had led, buried deep in the English countryside, since he had brought me back scarce half-alive to Malfine, which was then masterless.

On that fine morning, there were the Salukis and myself clattering through the entrance-hall, and there was Belos, bearing a tray with silver coffee-pot and accoutrements, emerging from the region of the kitchens and making for the morning room. He danced neatly through the animals and sailed into the room in uncannily dignified fashion.

The long morning room we had fitted up a little since Elisabeth's arrival, that is to say, it had been swept, the pier glasses were cleared of grime, and new hangings of almond-green silk were spoken of, at least between Elisabeth and Belos. The coffee was placed on a table before a small tapestry sofa where faded roses and puffed-out cherubs gallivanted, and here Elisabeth took her seat and prepared to pour, while I admired the chestnut glint of her hair and the turn of her white neck. Her long legs were promisingly outlined in the satiny folds of her dress as it settled over her thighs with a soft *glissade.* But I bowed to convention and did not follow my inclinations. At least, not there and then.

"Belos, tell me of Kean's funeral rites at Richmond," said I. "Was it an occasion of high drama?"

"Oh yes, my lord! One of the most splendid productions ever witnessed—they must have rehearsed for days! After all, he was the greatest actor of our time; there's no disputing that, though he had many envious rivals, of course. But it could not have been better planned than if Mr. Kean had stage-managed it himself. The coffin was on public view in Mr. Kean's house before the ceremony so that all the mourners might file past and pay tribute, and then it was accompanied to the church by such a procession! Beadles, mutes, pages, walking along—all in the most sumptuous black—and the carriage-horses plumed, of course! And the actors—why, all the leading members of the profession were in attendance. Macready himself was one of the pall-bearers. And there were first-rate people from all the London theatres, from Drury Lane and Covent Garden and Sadler's Wells."

"And the music?" inquired Elisabeth. "Was there not beautiful music played upon the organ at such an occasion?"

There was a sadness in her voice; perhaps she thought for a moment, as did I, of the perfunctory funeral we had recently attended, of a man far from home, for whom there had been few expressions of grief. Odd, how things impress themselves upon our minds. It was perhaps the friendless nature of the rites for young Kelsoe that operated on my mind.

But Belos was answering Elisabeth. "Oh yes, the most solemn notes of Purcell and Handel—and singers from the opera, in such fine voice, too! It was a great spectacle, I can tell you that. And I met many acquaintances . . ."

His voice seemed to hesitate here. There was something more, I thought. Was there an undercurrent of regret in his words? They say acting is a fever in the blood—an infection that can never be thrown off, the taste for that tawdry, lionized, dangerous existence. Yet, looking at Belos' quiet exterior, who would think he had such a longing in him?

Speculation was suspended. There suddenly came such a menagerie of cries from the farther end of the room—of spitting and howling and barking—that further conversation was impossible and I jumped up to investigate.

The heavy brocade swathes at one of the tall windows appeared to be in motion—indeed, to be boiling with activity. Beneath it, Nubia and Taharka were leaping frantically, their claws shredding great rents in the old silk, and Taharka's nose appeared to have a bloody scratch upon it. Suddenly, at the top of the curtains, was a fantasmagorical black shape, hissing and spitting and scurrying up to the safety of the pole, where it sat and contemplated the bounding furies below.

"Good God, where did this come from?"

Belos advanced swiftly down the room, giving a discreet over-butlerish sort of cough that was an inadequate comment upon the turbulent scenario.

The cat moved—no, that is too commonplace a verb—it positively liquefied down and leaped on Belos' shoulder, where it dug its claws in, while the dogs pressed about, yet sensing that their quarry was now safe, and making no further serious pursuit.

"This is Cordillo, my lord."

"Cordillo? Belos, explain yourself."

"Edmund Kean's cat, my lord."

For once wordless, I flung myself down on a sofa and gestured for explanation.

"When I took my place with the others who went to file around the great man's coffin, I saw the cat hiding in the empty grate. You could scarce make it out, of course, just two eyes were to be seen, staring out of the blackness. I asked one of the beadles standing near the coffin about it, and he tried to give the creature a crack with his stick—'nasty evil thing,' he called it. Then he told me the story. 'Mr. Kean had the cat just before he died, and since then it's been lurking nearby—everyone says it's brought ill luck.' He called for a housemaid to chase it out, but the animal retreated to the interior of the grate and would have made to climb up inside the chimney. 'I'll light the fire and smoke it out,' says the maid. 'We've never fed it, but it won't go away—horrid beast that it is!' And she went off to fetch some coals, but I ran after her. 'Don't trouble yourself,' said I. 'Give me an old basket or something of the sort.' So she found me an old wicker creel, the kind that fishermen use, and I baited my trap with a scrap of meat."

"Belos, you deliberately caught this . . . this panther?"

"Yes, my lord, although you exaggerate as always."

"Yes, Ambrose, it is very true, you do. Panther, indeed!" This was from Elisabeth. "But, Belos, do proceed."

"Very well, madam. The cat would not have come into the trap for the meat alone; he came and snuffed at my hand first, and then quite quietly went into the basket, like a tame creature. So I took him to the funeral with me, putting the creel under a pew, and he was quiet as a black saint, except for howling a little with the hymns, but so did Madame Scaglini from the Theatre Royal who was standing nearby, so what was one wail the more? No one noticed anything amiss, at any rate."

"And then you brought the creature back to Malfine. Belos, has it not occurred to you what a menagerie I have assembled here already? There is Zaraband, there are the dogs, there is Miss Westmorland's old pony—why do you suppose I should add to my woes with this heathen creature?"

"Surely there is no shortage of space, my lord?"

This was impossible to deny, considering the vast acreage of Malfine.

"Kean was a great animal-lover; I heard he kept a pet lion at one time."

This was from Elisabeth, who had risen from the table.

"I suppose we must be thankful we do not have Leo running through the galleries here."

Belos evidently took this as a sign of weakening and pressed his advantage.

"And Cordillo will keep to my room, my lord, if you desire it."

"It is not so much what I desire, Belos, as what the dogs will find bearable. And what did you say of ill luck? Did this animal not bring bad fortune upon its previous owner?"

A voice from the other end of the room intervened. "Shame on you, Ambrose, if you let superstition guide your actions! Let reason prevail!"

Elisabeth was in the act of pouring cream into a saucer. Clearly, the cause was lost.

But I had been right in one respect. There was something more that Belos had acquired at Richmond, apart from a great black monster of a cat, although it was not at all what I had expected to hear.

After dinner that evening, he and I were on the terrace overlooking the sweep of overgrown lawn, and Belos resumed his account of what had happened at Edmund Kean's funeral. He told me of the—I almost called it a party—it was, of course, the assembly of the mourners after the funeral, the grand equivalent of the subdued little gathering in the gloomy hall at Jesmond Place.

From Belos' words, I formed the picture of a most lively group, not at all funereal, a sea of lustrous raven silks and satins, along with sable ostrich trimmings, umbrageous lace mantles, tenebrous pelisses and sweeping cloaks of deepest sooty velvet. Thus, somberly yet bravely clad, members of the theatrical profession who had not seen one another for years came together. Broken Dogberries, aged

Capulets, who had been touring with small companies from Glasgow to Brecon, great Portias who had played at Drury Lane and Covent Garden, several elderly Hamlets—a confusion of Kembles—all, it seemed, had kissed and chattered and trilled and boomed in one feathery befrilled froth that spilled out of the church and through the streets of Richmond.

"And under a tiny crepuscular chapeau peeped the delicate face of Miss Fanny Kemble, Juliet to the life—"

"I hope not to the death, Belos."

"It was a most serious occasion, and perhaps your lordship will be pleased to refrain from your customary levity."

"I'm sorry, Belos. What was it, 'crepuscular chapeau . . .'? Oh yes—she had a black bonnet. Do proceed."

"My lord, I happened to mention something to a friend—an actor whom I knew before I left these shores for Greece, who had some success at the Theatre Royal in Bristol and also traveled to Richmond for the funeral. We had paused for a drink in a tavern near the river, and I told him of Malfine and my present position."

Here I half-expected Belos to say that he had been persuaded to return to the theatrical life, that he had succumbed to the lure of the flaring lights and the grease-paint, but this was not what transpired.

"We recounted our experiences in those years since we had last met—he had some success, I believe, as the juvenile lead in the plays of Mr. Sheridan—and as I was telling him of my new life here, I mentioned that I was not required at home for a few days, because my master had betaken himself to stay at Jesmond Place.

" 'Jesmond?' said he. 'Now where have I heard that name before?'

" 'It is an old West Country name,' I answered.

" 'No, I mean I am sure I have heard it in another connection—to do with our profession. But I cannot now recall what it was. Perhaps someone else at the Theatre Royal might recollect it.'

"Well, he racked his brains, but could not then remember, and it is rather surprising he could recall anything at all, so fine were the hospitalities and the entertainments of the occasion. However, I mention it to your lordship; rather an odd incident, was it not?"

"Yes, it was indeed, Belos. What on earth could such a quiet old-established family as the Jesmonds have to do with the theatre? As for Lady Jesmond, I believe Sir Antony did marry out of the usual circle of suitable country cabbages, but he found her, I believe, in an inn."

I brushed this away, without thinking more of it, so taken was I by Belos' account of the mourners. All the more discredit to me. One should never be so seduced by gorgeous language as to miss a hard little grain lurking in its lustrous depths. And something beyond that, lying deeper still than the small nugget of fact: a shade of feeling on the part of the speaker which I, preoccupied as I was by levity at the account of the preposterous funereal splendors, missed at the time. I found it only in retrospect, when I considered that conversation later on, after the many troubles and fears engendered by the strange events which I now relate.

When I rode out next morning, I should perhaps have turned Zaraband's head toward Bristol and made some theatrical inquiries, but regrettably I did not attach enough weight to what Belos had told me. Instead, we went in the clear contrary direction.

We took the road to Oxford.

Part Two

OXFORD INTERLUDE

CHAPTER 11

NOW, I know it is the fashion for men such as I, Ambrose Malfine, that is to say, those of wealth and background, to indulge in cheerful reminiscence of their college days, to speak with fondness of "m'tutor," or of the college pastimes, such as playing cricket for velvet caps, or throwing feather-beds into fountains, or piddling in the Sheldonian Theatre. I cannot join in such a chorus, since I lasted but one term at the University, and then high-tailed it overseas like the scamp I was.

In short, I ran away.

I cast the dust of Oxford from off my feet.

And I have never before nor afterward made such a wise and sensible decision, no, not if I had studied upon it for a twelvemonth altogether and consulted all the philosophers in the kingdom. Nothing in my education has ever done me anything like as much good as the running away from it.

On this fine morning, I grant you, Oxford was a city from which none but an idiot would desire ever to depart, much less exchange for the violent and savage world within which I had become deep immersed scarce one month after quitting the venerable spires. While my contemporaries were nesting in their ancient collegiate dreys and burrows, while they were enjoying the scholarly pursuits proper to their station, *viz,* whores and waxwork shows, bawds, balls and boxing-matches, Livy and lotteries, dice, Diodorus and drunkenness, I was learning quite a different trade.

I had been a young man full of ideals, which even now have power to seize my brain and grip my heart, though fighting for them nearly killed me. I had enlisted in a heroic struggle, the fight of Greece for independence, and found my learning must be of butchery and treachery, not Theodorus but throat-cutting, hunger instead of Hesiod. The study of anatomy, however, was much in evidence. I became practiced in chirurgery: that of slitting living arteries. The penalty for failure in those particular examinations was death.

I scraped a pass.

I have, of course, at one time or another, studied the more usual academic subjects, but although in my wandering quest for knowledge I sat at the feet of scholars from Prague to Salonika, there was one particular area of study which now explained my unsentimental journey to my alma mater. For there was something about the deaths of those two young men at Jesmond Place which could perhaps be resolved by this expedition—and resolve the mystery I must: otherwise Elisabeth would forever be uneasy concerning the welfare of Lady Jesmond. Already, I had perceived, Elisabeth was torn between her feelings for me and her loyalty to her new-found friend—for so, it appeared, Clara Jesmond had become, having progressed from the role of Miss

Anstruther's mere employer through her very vulnerability, which my dear and warmly-disposed beloved evidently pitied with her tender and affectionate heart.

And so, by many a twining and turning, I found myself this morning, descending Headington Hill toward the city which I had quit so many years ago.

Zaraband and I had stopped the night at Wheatley, a place of nothing but inns, serving the travelers between London and Oxford. I desired to catch a glimpse of the city from Shotover Hill, and we approached it over the packed red soil of the roadway through what remained of an ancient forest, still coppiced by the colleges for their timber. Footpads were said to haunt the lower slopes of Shotover, along with the foxes, and I had heard a story once that Shelley sailed a toy ship on the black water filling the ugly old claypits dug deep into its sides. He must, like myself, have played truant from his studies, although unlike myself he did not quit Oxford of his own volition.

But there was the city, spread out before us in the morning sun, the silvery twiddles and fiddles of the towers all sharp and clear against the sky, and in the distance, the faint sounds of clocks striking. They were all pell-mell out of time, as Alexander Pope noticed a century or so ago, and contradicted one another in their melodious voices, but one might discern that it was round about ten o'clock in the morning, give or take a quarter-hour or so.

Ten o'clock in the morning! Now that's the time for youth to leave off the revels of the previous night and set about recovery, for now is the season of the parties and balls, the picnics and pleasures of long grass. Indeed, as I rode down Headington Hill, I saw there were still some bleary-eyed youths strolling toward the city, with one or two women in gauzy dresses that had ill withstood the rigors of the previous night. The Headington alehouse known as Louse Hall was still in operation, I presumed.

I had almost a mind to call in and drink a bumper or two with Mother Louse, for old times' sake, but the damnable conscience of maturity made me—not forswear—but at least postpone it.

Over Magdalen Bridge we went, a youth crying out, "That's a fine horse, sir!" as we passed, and we made our way up the High Street and thence turned down St. Aldate's, with Wren's great gateway on the left, remembered as if in a dream from the days of my youth.

For there at Christ Church had I been entered, as a nobleman scholar, with a gold tassel upon my mortar-board, with my own servant and my cellar. I was sixteen years of age, and eager for everything, and my guardians, distant family cousins, did not deny me what was considered appropriate to my rank and wealth. So I had an allowance of five hundred a year, a set of rooms overlooking Tom Quad with my own furniture and china, and four dozen bottles of wine, and a dozen each of port, sherry, claret and Madeira. How clearly I remember the wine-merchant's bill!

It took me, as a young man, a little time to discover that what I sought was not to be found in Oxford. This process of elimination started at Christ Church, where "m'tutor," an affable mouse who slept curled up on cushions for much of the day, attended on me sometimes and begged me to read a little Virgil, which I occasionally condescended to do. Once or twice I visited anatomy lectures, where I usually found some Dutchman hacking dogs about to little purpose. There was, I recall, a pig-pen maintained outside the Divinity School, which received the bones discarded after the anatomy lessons.

I would probably have sunk into the dull and barbaric amusements of my contemporaries, keeping a bear in my rooms and so forth—at the highest, performing in private theatricals or publishing my own poetry. Or perhaps I should have emulated the vasty indolence of my teachers, had I not been possessed of a disposition which naturally recoiled from such tedium, and had the good fortune to meet the personage whom I purposed to see now, on this visit of my older self to the haunts of youth.

But it would have to wait till later, for he was not to be found in Christ Church. I entered beneath the tower of that over-built and pompous foundation, greeted the porter with my name and asked for a guest-room and a place in the stables for my horse, and watched with some amusement while that stout luminary bestirred himself and sent for a comrade out of the Old Tom tavern for support. "I don't think, my lord, you will see anything changed since you were in residence, though there have been terrible goings-on in that little place across the road." (He meant Pembroke College, which lies just the other side of St. Aldate's.) "I do hear tell they are making their Fellows pass their examinations! Would never do here—this is a gentleman's college, I say. Hey, Jenkins! This old member of the House is none other than a lordship, so stir your stumps, now!"

Oxford dearly loves a lord!

A few coins changed hands—to be exact, from my palm to his. And then, arrangements made, I crossed the road, to the poorest place in Oxford.

"Is Dr. Twiddie in the College?"

Even the porter of Pembroke looked half-starved. The place was tiny, a huddle of rooms round a cramped courtyard and a few unsavory lodging-houses. Nevertheless, it had been in this rabbit-warren that I had discovered the one shining light of my Oxford career, the sole source of any intellectual aspirations which inspired me to open a book or a set of tables.

From time to time we had corresponded, but not since my return from Greece. For aught he knew, I was dead and mouldering in a Levantine grave or providing food for oriental fishes.

I dashed in under the Pembroke College gateway, where Samuel Johnson had once lodged. He too had made a return visit to the scene of his youthful studies: I recollect being told by an old college servant that the great doctor had grown so large he had to be pushed up the winding stair to the rooms he had occupied as a student. The college seemed to be reviving itself, however: I saw with surprise that the Chapel appeared to be in some process of repair. What dreary times are overtaking Oxford!

The staircase I had been wont to climb, one which led off the courtyard, was however as rotten as ever: one day, the timbers would give way and one of the finest brains in the country would be precipitated to its end down a stairwell.

I banged upon the inner door of the set of rooms. The outer stood open, probably too warped to be properly shut. There was a shuffling within, and then someone was peering up at me, someone whose head was about level with my shoulder.

"Why, Ambrose Malfine! I feared you were lost to us forever!"

I gazed at Dr. William Twiddie, whose name had been

such a source of mirth to the young bloods. Doubtless, the jokes and laughter on that name still echoed round the quads of Oxford, and doubtless they were still ignored with the matchless serenity of its possessor.

Inside, the room was a shock, to one who knew Oxford. It was in immaculate order, with rows of bookshelves neatly arrayed with volumes clean and well-dusted, and piles of paper tidily stacked on a huge desk. At the far end of the room was a long table, fitted up with all kinds of glass pipes and retorts and small burners, where again the sense of order and cleanliness prevailed.

"Well, Ambrose, you had a mighty quick mind, so I am not surprised you have returned to us. Do you intend to take up studying again?"

"No, I fear I must disappoint you! But I have come to ask you for information, for you are the most knowledgable man in England on the topic which I have in mind."

The Fellows of Oxford colleges are not noted for bashfulness, and even Twiddie placed truth above modesty.

"Now that poor Beddoes is dead—but you will have heard of that?"

"Yes, but I was away from home for many years, Dr. Twiddie. I confess I know little of what has passed here."

"Ah yes, you went to Greece, did you not? I recall you were a regular young fire-eater—a real revolutionary spirit. Those were stirring times! I recollect Dr. Beddoes—the best chemist we ever had—he went off to France; he was all for the Jacobins, yet I fancy he was disappointed in them. At any rate, I account him the finest scientific brain of his time. He left Oxford, you know—but he died, he died! Ah, I am older and the young men are younger, as it seems to me."

There was a melancholy sigh as he said this. How sad,

thought I, to be always greeting new pupils, to feel oneself every year older and older in regard to them!

"And Dr. Henderson? Was he not a friend of Beddoes?"

"Ah, he is gone, too! And there were the strangest rumors . . ."

I had heard of some of them. John Henderson had been an exceptionally gifted Fellow of the college, though before my time. Not the least of his talents was a remarkable facility in languages, so that he spoke Arabic, Hebrew, Latin, and could assume not merely a language but the dialect of any locality in Europe, so that he could pass for an inhabitant. When I had become a student in Oxford, I had desired to learn, not the classical Greek which could be spouted by the line by any jackass who had his arse whipped, but the Cretan dialect spoken on my mother's island.

Already, it seems to me now as I look back, I must have formed some idea of going thither, to the windswept castle of Mala Fina on its rocky promontory, where lay my Cretan inheritance. I stumbled toward it, as you might say, and as a new student in Oxford I inquired me out some guidance for my footsteps.

And met with such remarks as, "Ah, you should have been here in Henderson's day, for he knew the Greek of the islands! And there is no one now in Oxford who could teach you. Why should we be interested in what the peasants speak nowadays?"

Henderson's departure had been Oxford's loss. He was, for example, as well as a linguist, a considerable medical man, and a charitable one as well; in a fever epidemic he had sold one of his treasured books to buy drugs for the treatment of the poor. His science, I knew, displayed the same genius as the rest of his talents. I wondered, now, what had become of him.

"Where did Henderson go? Is he dead or alive?"

"In a manner of speaking, both, some say. None knows quite where he went, except that he disappeared, if that is what you might call it, some years ago."

"What can you mean, Dr. Twiddie?"

"There were strange stories . . . but I am being very inhospitable, Ambrose. Why do not you take a turn with me in the Summer Common Room, and have some refreshment?"

Pembroke College did not abolish all old customs, as has lately been the fashion in some colleges, in favor of more virtuous practices. It has retained its comfortable old sitting room perched on the ancient Town Wall, and it was with some pleasure that I entered into it after some twenty years' absence. It is a low paneled room, with some fly-blown prints and musty portraits upon the walls, and small circular tables dotted about, their surfaces marked unaffectedly with rings. Here we now took our seats, Dr. Twiddie calling out as we passed the buttery, and I shortly perceived that the Fellows still kept a damned good claret.

"Ah, poor Henderson," sighed the good old Twiddie, his thoughts evidently still running on his former colleague.

I sipped, pausing to think about that whimsical creature. "He often went to bed at daybreak, as I was told, and rose in the afternoon," said I.

Twiddie responded more sharply than I might have expected. His head came up suddenly from his glass of claret, and he looked at me with his small shrewd periwinkle eyes.

"Aye, it may be from that custom of his that some of the stories began."

"Stories? He was always eccentric . . ." I had in mind the wild extravagant tales still circulating in the college in the days of my youth—that Dr. Henderson had once forgotten to eat for five whole days, that he always slept in a wet shirt. Yet Twiddie's tone had implied something more than these affectionately-regarded quirks.

"Yes, there were things whispered all over Oxford—oh, that was a few years before your time, of course. We took good care they should not come to the ears of the students."

"What kind of whispers?"

Twiddie shifted on the worn cushions of the chair.

"That he . . . well, it is absurd . . . they said that he had communion with . . ."

"What, he took up Christianity?"

"No, do not jest . . . that he had communion with ghostly powers. That he sought to speak with the dead."

"Good God! A Fellow of an Oxford college!"

"Yes, and one who had been a leading scientific brain of his generation. But some of his own actions gave rise to that kind of talk, you know—he was himself partly to blame. He looked at books that had scarcely been opened since the Middle Ages."

"Perhaps any scientist might meet with such accusations, if he delves into uncommon studies?"

"Yes, and it is true that he went far into the byways of knowledge—and also that he was apt to take large drafts of something more than ordinary inspiration . . ."

Twiddie coughed. I had forgotten that comfortable Oxford habit of hinting at another's vices.

"He was a drunkard, you would say."

"Well, perhaps that construction might be placed . . . he was not always inebriated, you know. Just . . . upon occasion."

"Sometimes upon important occasion?"

"In a word, yes. But, Ambrose, he had a reputation for something far worse . . ."

"For what, pray? Ravishing the college cook? Selling the silver plate? Come on, Twiddie, tell me. I can scarce contain myself!"

"No, sir, I'll say no more. No doubt the poor fellow is long dead and I'll not speak ill of him."

And I could not draw him further on the subject.

CHAPTER 12

THE information I had received about Dr. Henderson was fascinating, but it was not what I had come to Oxford to hear. I was there, in fact, to make a particular inquiry of the most advanced men of modern science, whose mastery of a certain subject should exceed that of any in Europe.

Twiddie and I were comfortably seated in the King's Arms, to which tavern we seemed to have repaired for lunch by almost unnoticeable degrees, ambling up St. Aldate's for a breath of air, and so strolling, talking, idling along till our appetites were sharpened, we found ourselves at a table, opposite a large cold roast and a black flagon or two.

On the way, in the Broad there was a woman with a painted face came up and clapped her arms about me and swore she had once been hauled up into my rooms through the window, but, oh St. Peter! I denied her as a matter of policy if not of forgetfulness. I did not wish to lose Twiddie's company.

So, when we had safely 'scaped the avenging harpy and

scuttled along into the tavern, I broached to Twiddie the purpose of my visit.

"Ah, now that is a most interesting chemical question!"

"I had thought that you, sir, as one of the leading experts in the study of chemistry, might be able to assist me. It is in connection with the decease of a young man."

"Well, it is very good of you to take the bonds of friendship so faithfully, Ambrose."

I had not actually lied, of course.

Twiddie went on: "But, as a matter of fact, I am not the authority on the subject. The person you seek is Professor Daubeny—he is the Professor of Chemistry. But I could introduce you to him."

"Oh, that would answer the case exactly! Then I would have the pleasure of consulting you *and* Professor Daubeny together—two great scientific minds at once!"

"Very well, I'll send a note inviting him to dine with us this evening."

Paper, ink and a quill were soon obtained and the potboy dispatched, returning very shortly afterward with a handsome letter of thanks.

"But, Ambrose, will you not tell me what this is all about?"

"Dr. Twiddie, if you will walk with me down the High Street, I will begin the story on my way. I have a particular errand to perform which I fancy will advance my present studies considerably."

The day continued warm, the scents of lilac and early roses drifting over old gray walls from sheltered college gardens as we walked. What a very fine city is Oxford, when there are no tiresome scholastic duties to perform!

"I wish to call in here, Dr. Twiddie, if you please."

"Very well, Ambrose."

The good doctor sounded rather puzzled, as indeed he might, for we had stopped at a jeweler's shop, the window displaying chiefly some pieces of silver, as a snuff-box with the arms of the University, gilt labels for wine-decanters, and the like.

Bellamy & Son. Suppliers of fine plate to the Gentry and Nobility. The engraving of coats-of-arms a speciality.

We entered beneath the sign. The shop was small and dark, belying the rather grand exterior, but the shopkeeper was as obsequious as his signboard implied, rushing forth and bowing low.

"Will it please your worships to take a chair? In what way may I be permitted to assist your lordship?"

I wondered how the devil he had recognized me and then apprehended that this was his usual mode of address to a potential customer. Groveling raises in me a powerful desire to kick the perpetrator, but I desisted.

"There is nothing I desire to purchase, but there is something I wish you to perform for me."

"Oh, indeed, any service at all, my lord, any service . . . what a handsome flask!"

It was Cyriack Jesmond's hip-flask. The late Cyriack Jesmond, I should say.

Dr. Twiddie gazed on in astonishment.

"But not made here, my lord. West Country workmanship, I should say. Why, here is the Exeter hallmark."

The little man knew his business. As he peered at the flask, he had lifted it near to his face, and commencing to unscrew the top, sniffed at it curiously.

"But what has been in it? Not just the cognac which is ordinarily placed in a gentleman's hip-flask, I think. Now what does your worship want me to do with it? Do you wish me to dispose of it? I think I could name you a fair price . . ."

"No, no. What I want you to do, Mr. Bellamy, is to cut it open. But first, kindly supply me with a small flask into which I may pour the dregs left in this."

"Cut it open, sir? So that the inside is exposed?"

Well, yes, that had been my intention and I intimated as much.

Bellamy (or his father) was used to the whims of gentlemen, however strange. "Very well, sir, it will take but a few minutes. I have my tools at the back here. Would it please you to wait."

The drops of brownish liquid left in the bottom of young Cyriack's hip-flask were soon decanted into a small crystal bottle, which I placed in my pocket.

Then we sat in Bellamy's (or his son's) chairs, listening to the grinding of a wheel cutting through soft metal, and he shortly hurried back, with the flask in two halves, as neat as if it had been an oyster-shell broken apart. The smell now hung heavily in the air of the little shop.

"Why, sir, here is a strange mark on the inside . . . almost like the remains of a blister, is it not?"

It was indeed, and there appeared, though in the dim light of the shop I could not be certain, to be a few tiny bright splinters embedded in it.

I gave the jeweler a generous tip for the crystal bottle and his services. Then, seizing a kerchief which the surprised Dr. Twiddie had happened to produce from his pocket, and wrapping the halves of the flask in it, I accompanied the scholar back to Carfax and thence to his rooms in Pembroke College.

Professor Daubeny arrived that evening to dine with us. My feelings toward Oxford were softened by its bright beauty in this gentle weather, especially as I had taken Zaraband out for a gallop in the afternoon. Our course, lying as it did along the riverbank to Wolvercote and Port Meadow, was dappled with the moving silvery lights of willow, and a thousand purple-blue dragonflies skimmed over the surface of the water. Here and there on the banks were little parties of young bloods, almost released from their studies, for this was the final term of the year and the dreamy sleep of the long vacation would begin ere long. Once or twice I saw a solitary student reading under a tree, with the enchanted deep absorption that almost makes one desire the scholar's life.

Yet I was not so sunk in love with Oxford, neither, that I forgot to make inquiry as to kitchen provisions, intimating that if Twiddie desired to order a special dinner in his rooms, I would meet any monetary deficiencies. I was reassured by Dr. Twiddie's description of our menu. "I have inquired out what delicacies may be provided and we are to have cod in caper sauce, roast beef, and pigeons with asparagus," he reported. "With a jelly pyramid to follow."

Admittedly, the good doctor then added with irrepressible excitement, "Oh, and what do you think? *Trotter pie*!"

Well, I had to allow him some indulgence. At least it was a better menu than those damned cold collops at Jesmond Place.

Professor Daubeny proved a brisk fellow, and I came quickly to the point, after the dishes had been cleared away. We sat with a decanter of port, but my two companions showed no signs of the vast imbibing that I recalled was universal in the days of my youth. I fancy moral reform is spreading its gray little tentacles into every peaceful crevice and strangling the natural debaucheries of youth.

At any rate, when I placed the two halves of the silver hip-flask upon the table, both chemists were quite clear-headed and, as we had not lit tobacco pipes, it was quite noticeable that there was still a whiff of the smell upon which the jeweler had commented. "It seems to be emanating chiefly from this," commented Daubeny.

He tapped the curious adhesion upon the inside of the flask—an uneven ring, oval in shape, about half an inch across, and of a thick jellyish substance.

I did not prompt him. "And I would say," he continued, "though it is a strange thing in a gentleman's hip-flask, yet once one has experienced this odor one can never mistake it—I would say it is the smell of prussic acid!"

"But that is a deadly poison!"

"Yes, Lord Ambrose. But there are tests one can perform that would make absolutely certain that prussic acid had been present."

"Could you undertake those tests, Professor Daubeny? Upon the liquid in this small bottle and also upon this mark here on the inside of the hip-flask?"

"Yes, certainly. Come to my laboratory tomorrow, if you will."

Dr. Twiddie, who had been staring at the two shining halves of what must be undoubtedly a curious instrument of death, now looked at us across the table in horror, as he took in the implications of what he saw.

"So somebody must have put prussic acid in here, in order to commit murder! Imagine, the owner of this flask takes but a swallow—and death is instantaneous, as if he were felled by an axe!"

"No, as a matter of fact, Twiddie, that is not always the case. There is sometimes a slight interval between taking the poison and the onset of the symptoms."

"What do you mean, exactly, Professor?" I leaned forward in my anxiety to hear what he replied.

"Well, there have been cases where the deceased was able to behave quite normally for a few minutes after swallowing prussic acid. It is generally believed, even among the medical profession, that the acid immediately takes effect as soon as it has been swallowed, yet that does not always happen. Indeed, there was a young man falsely accused of murder on that account."

"Pray tell us the circumstances!"

Twiddie now was as eager as I. Evidently, the phenomenon of which Daubeny was about to speak was not well-known, even among leading men of science.

"Oh yes, there was an inquest a few years ago upon a young woman by the name of Buswell—Judith Buswell, if my memory serves me. A young man called Foster was charged with her murder; for it appeared at first that she could not have committed suicide. She was found lying in bed with the bedclothes smoothly pulled up to her breast, her arms neatly crossed. At her side, under the sheet, lay the bottle which had contained the acid—with the cork firmly replaced in the neck. It was assumed that she could not have performed those acts herself—and yet, gentlemen, consider how little time really is required to perform them. Time is so illusory, is it not? We take the significance of actions to be somehow a measure of the time they take to carry out—but reflect upon how many things may be performed in a few seconds, and yet how important may be the consequences of those actions, of those brief moments. Even as I have been speaking, there has been time to kill a man, has there not?"

It was true. Life is so quick, so easy, to extinguish. A man can have a dagger run through his back and gasp out his bloody lungs in a few seconds. I had killed a man in the time it took old Twiddie now to stretch across and reach for his pipe.

Sitting in that Oxford room, surrounded by the darkness of a summer's night, the leavings of an affable meal scattered companionably upon the table, I knew that death, however terrible, however devilish, may be accomplished by a cool hand in less time than it takes to crack a nut.

But it was not murder that Daubeny had in mind in his present considerations. He continued with his explanation.

"It was demonstrated at the trial of Foster that five to eight seconds would have sufficed for the unfortunate woman to have placed the stopper in the neck of the bottle after she had swallowed the contents, and for her to assume the position in bed in which she was found. And persons may certainly continue to move about for a brief time after taking the poison—that is now known beyond a doubt. There was an instance in which the symptoms did not come on for a full quarter of an hour. I'm afraid that the notion that the moment prussic acid is taken, death is instantaneous, is a fallacy."

"What happened to Foster?" I inquired.

"Oh, he was acquitted. And there have been other cases—there was a young man in Germany who was found in bed with two empty vials of the acid, one on each side of the bed, and no other container in sight. So he evidently was able to take one vial and then the other and to place both neatly beside him before he was overcome."

This discussion should have been reassuring with regard to the recent tragedies at Jesmond Place: if young Dr. Kelsoe had indeed taken his own life, then we could assume that a murderer was not on the loose in that ill-assorted household.

But then how must we suppose that Cyriack Jesmond met his death?

"Professor Daubeny, I should be greatly in your debt if you will carry out the tests for detecting the presence of prussic acid. I will call on you at your laboratory tomorrow, if I may."

CHAPTER 13

I breakfasted in Christ Church, taking it in the guest-room which had been allotted to me rather than at the Fellows' table. I could not forget the sight of that magnificent hall, adorned with portraits and gilt plate, and at the end of the high table a disgusting open dish of bones and scraps into which the nasty old creatures threw their leavings. It had repelled me as a student, and, peering into the hall as I descended the great staircase, I saw that the custom had not changed.

I went for a short walk to get a burst of morning air in my lungs, turning toward the river; some of the landmarks of this place I had quite forgotten, and some now came back to me. There was Folly Bridge, for instance, with the grog shops clustered beyond it, and this decayed tower on the riverbank—why, that was something to do with old Twiddie's conversation, surely . . . What was it?

The great clock of Tom Tower broke into my thoughts as

it sounded the hour. Time to walk back for my meeting with Daubeny.

My long legs took me briskly up the steps in front of the Ashmolean Museum, and I made my way down into the basement, where science held its sway. The long wooden benches of Professor Daubeny's laboratory were much cleaner than the college dining-tables, stained though they were with burns and deposits from various chemicals. Neatly arrayed were the glistening glass and metal vessels of his mysteries: the sirens, the Magdeburg Hemisphere, the ghostly glass cylinder of the Guinea-and-Feather, by means of which, as I recalled, I had seen demonstrated the resistance of air to falling bodies. A pungent, sulfurous whiff filled the air as I struggled to recall some of the terms I had learned. Was that green glass contrivance not a retort, and surely that was a dropping bottle, for measuring minute quantities of poison?

Daubeny himself was holding up a small beaker, the sides of which were coated with white.

"Ah, Malfine! Yes, this is the result of the test I have performed with nitrate of silver—by washing the sides of the hip-flask with a little water and then adding the water to a beaker containing the nitrate. You see the white film formed thereby? That is a sure indication of the presence of prussic acid, even in a dilute solution. And I have obtained the same result from the liquid in the little bottle which you gave me—though there, it was more marked. There is another test which I wish to carry out—do take a seat and observe."

Like any student, I took a seat upon the bench and watched Daubeny's hands as he scraped off the small patch of odd blisterlike matter from the surface of the inside of the flask. He placed it briefly under a microscope. He was a contradiction in terms, a fierce little man, square-jawed and forceful-looking, yet with a Cupid's bow of a mouth and the delicate hands of a watchmaker.

"Yes, now I can see—there are tiny sherds of fine glass in this, Malfine. As if an ampoule has been broken. Look down this microscope."

I peered down the tiny channels of brass and saw for myself: glittering fragments of sharp light, stuck in some thick grayish substance.

Then he carefully placed the scrapings in a beaker, poured in a little water and swirled it around, and then carefully poured off the liquid. He then allowed a few drops to fall into another glass, which he told me contained the nitrate, and I saw for myself the white deposit forming within.

"Again—prussic acid," he observed. "Though I cannot be certain: there may be some contamination from the waxy substance which I scraped from the side of the flask. Nor, of course, do I know the nature of the dregs of brown liquid in your small vial—though it has the odor of some kind of brandy."

"Yes, that will very probably have been the case. But tell me, Professor Daubeny, could you not hazard a guess as to the nature of the curious blister, or ampoule, or whatever it was, that might have been in the flask?"

Daubeny evidently did not care for hazard. But he responded, though slowly, tucking his black cravat into his waistcoat as he considered.

"Well now, if I were forced to make a guess, I should say that this was wax—ordinary household candle wax, in which there has been embedded, for some extraordinary reason, a glass capsule of the kind that medical men sometimes use to contain . . ."

He stopped, and looked at me, and then continued.

"To contain a small quantity of a very strong drug. Such as a poison."

The web of the Jesmond Place entanglement drew tighter. What could be the reason for the deaths, by poison, of two apparently healthy young men? They had not even been resident at the same time—Cyriack had not returned to Jesmond Place till the body of young Kelsoe was about to be interred in its last resting-place. They could have been only briefly acquainted, before Cyriack's departure for the start of the summer term, so that they would have known each other for a matter of weeks. If Cyriack had been murdered—and so it would seem, from the extraordinary evidence that poison had been inserted into his hip-flask—then should I suppose that was the fate that had also befallen Kelsoe? Although, recalling Daubeny's stories of the unfortunates who had ended their own lives by means of prussic acid, we now had the testimony of no less than the Professor of Chemistry at Oxford that Kelsoe's death could have been suicide.

Yes, thought I, but the fact that Kelsoe could have died by his own hand, that Dr. Sandys might have been wrong in his conclusion that it was murder—this did not mean that Kelsoe was proved a suicide beyond all doubt. The possibility, not the certainty, was there.

And how had the poison operated, in the case of Cyriack?

I decided to acquaint Professor Daubeny with the full facts of Cyriack Jesmond's horrifying decease, witnessed by a small crowd of onlookers.

"Dear me, such a tragedy! But he was a student at my

college, you know—I recognize the name. I'm afraid he was not a very brilliant pupil, to say the least—though his father dabbled in science, so I was told by those who remembered him, from his student days thirty years ago. Yes, there are still a few gray-beards around who taught Jesmond senior. I never taught young Cyriack myself, but I recall that his tutor told me he paid no attention to his studies. Rather a violent disposition, too, I fancy. He has—or had, I should say—a reputation for brawling."

Brawling and perhaps worse. I thought of Cyriack as I had glimpsed him at Jesmond Place, his fist raised above the terrified face of Lady Jesmond.

It would not have been surprising to discover that someone had plotted the decease of Cyriack Jesmond. But who should have done so in the case of young Kelsoe?

"Professor Daubeny, from the curious circumstances here, from the splinters of glass and the waxy substance and so on—can you suggest what might have happened to Cyriack Jesmond?"

"This is purely conjecture, mind . . . but yes, this is what might—I say *might*—have happened. If a few drops of prussic acid—a very small quantity is enough to kill—were inserted in an ampoule of thin glass, and the opening of that ampoule temporarily stoppered with a waxy seal, or even one of crystalized sugar, then the sugar or wax would dissolve eventually—how long, of course, would depend on many factors, such as its thickness, the strength of the acid, and whether there was another liquid present on the outside. If the ampoule had been placed in a flask and brandy then poured in, then the spirit would act as a dissolving agent upon the seal. There would be perhaps a short respite—very brief, but, as in the cases I described to you, it might be enough to perform a few actions. Then, the death agony."

The memory came into my mind: Cyriack, leaping on the horse, taking a long pull from his flask . . . a few more seconds while the animal careered down the drive—and then Cyriack rearing up in the saddle, his body bent in a horrible unnatural bow as if he performed some grotesque circus trick.

I tried to picture what might have happened. A tiny glass capsule of poison, its mouth stoppered with a soluble adhesion. The murderer places this in Cyriack's own hip-flask, quietly awaiting its owner's return from Oxford. Cyriack calls for the flask to be filled . . .

"Would not the ampoule, as soon as brandy was poured into the flask, would it not float up—even perhaps bob up into the mouth of the flask, and the drinker would straight away detect something?"

For answer, Daubeny strode into his study adjacent to the laboratory and returned with a decanter about a third full which he placed upon the sulfurous laboratory bench.

I removed the stopper of the decanter and took a sniff.

"Good God, Daubeny, what are you thinking of? Conducting your experiments with the finest French cognac?"

Daubeny seemed rather put out. "I keep the brandy only for emergencies, you understand. To stimulate the heart in case of medical need."

"Too good to waste on keeping fools alive. Damned fine stuff, by the smell of it."

But Daubeny proceeded with his experiment. He took a candle, cut off a little wax which he melted in a spoon over a flame, and then from a drawer in a little brass and mahogany cabinet where it was set in a velvet trough like a ghostly fruit on a thin stem, he removed a gleaming bead of thin hollow glass.

Through the stem he poured a few drops of water, and then pressed the molten wax in the thin bore of the mouth so that it was sealed.

Then he dropped the ampoule into the cognac. We watched as it floated merrily on the golden surface. He tilted the decanter to pour a little into a glass and it instantly floated toward the opening, bobbing like a fisherman's buoy.

"Indeed, you were right, Malfine. It would be a very lucky chance that it should go unobserved—even if the potential victim were to take a deep gulp straight from the mouth of his hip-flask," observed the professor.

"That curious oval mark upon the side of the flask, which looks like the remains of a blister upon the skin," said I. "Can we account for that?"

For answer, the professor rang a bell, and a young boy appeared, with tousled hair and a leather apron.

"This is Simon," observed Daubeny. "He cleans out the laboratory—washes vessels and so forth. Simon, be so kind as to fetch me the silver jug from the pantry."

Simon ran off, Daubeny murmuring after him, "Wants to be a student—but a poor boy, yes, a poor boy. Oxford is not kind to poverty, as you will know, having studied here yourself."

I was ashamed to say that I did not know. I had taken no account of the servitors, poor students who slept in the attics and waited on the other students, struggling to study when they might. However, this was not the moment to dwell on the subject.

When Simon brought in the silver jug, Daubeny took it,

held a piece of wax inside it with a pair of tongs so that it was against the side, and then applied the flame of a candle to the outside in that place. The wax readily stuck to the inside of the jug, and Daubeny then inserted the ampoule and embedded it in the warm wax. There was a black smoky stain on the outside of the jug, where the flame of the candle had discolored it, but that was swiftly cleaned off with a piece of cloth.

"There," said Daubeny. "Now let me pour some brandy into it."

The liquid swirled into the jug. The ampoule remained obediently attached to the side of the vessel. "Of course, if the neck of the flask were very narrow, then one would have to use a piece of wire or something similar to hold the ampoule, instead of tongs, while one was maneuvering it into place—but that is really a minor matter. The wax would hold it in place for a while, at any rate. Depends on how thick it was."

Peering into the jug some fifteen minutes later, we saw the silvery bubble of glass come floating up amid the amber liquid. The trace of wax that had stoppered it had come out. If it had contained poison instead of a harmless drop of water, that would have drifted into the brandy. The glass was so thin that a jolt or a blow would have broken it before that happened, in any event. In which case, there would have been a few splinters of glass left in the ring of wax that had secured the ampoule to the side of the jug.

Exactly as had been the case with Cyriack Jesmond's hip-flask.

I returned to Christ Church to find that events had moved on since I had left the college. The porter was guarded, but managed to convey an extraordinary range of insinuations. His heavy eyebrows worked frantically up and down like signal-flags as he gave me the news.

"My lord, a personage has been inquiring for you—well, I suppose I must say two personages, only one . . ."

"Yes, man, out with it!"

"My lord, one was a woman!"

This word was whispered, but somehow it seemed to echo all the way round under Wren's great gateway.

"I'm suitably horrified. And the other, er . . . person?"

"Your lordship's butler, or so he says, though I never before heard of a butler who strode around like a gentleman!"

"Like an actor, if the truth be known."

"I beg your lordship's pardon?"

"Never mind, never mind. Tell me, where is this ill-assorted pair of creatures?"

"My lord, I requested them to wait in the Doctors' Parlor."

This was a little room near the entrance where the occasional female visitor was temporarily lodged in a kind of quarantine, so that she might not infect the rarefied world beyond with any nasty disease of reality. Hurrying through to it, I found Elisabeth and Belos, both with expressions of anxiety upon their faces, sitting uncomfortably upon a pair of worn old velvet chairs.

"Ambrose, Belos has learned something from his friend—"

"The actor, my lord, whom I mentioned to you, the old acquaintance whom I met at Kean's funeral. He has written to me now with news of such import . . ."

I recalled Belos' mention of his old friend. There had been some undercurrent to his tone, and I had interpreted it as a longing to return to the stage, but perhaps there had been more to it.

"We can take lunch in a private room over the Bear, just a few minutes away. Tell me over a meal, Belos. I'm quite famished by experimentation!"

"Yes, my lord."

Within a very short time, we were ensconced, as the sounds of rowdy undergraduates calling for ale drifted up the staircase of the inn, and a cold chicken was set before us, Elisabeth requesting a dish of young peas to be served with it. I gave the order for some accompaniments.

"Some hock, I fancy. And ice, landlord, if you have it."

"I'll send out for it, my lord."

"Excellent. Now, Belos!"

"The gist of the letter, my lord, concerns the Jesmond household. When Daniel—my acquaintance—when he returned to Bristol, he recollected some gossip and made inquiries. It seems that it was old news in the Theatre Royal at Bristol, but not entirely forgotten."

Belos leaned forward and his magnificent stage whisper shivered through the inn.

"My lady Jesmond is the daughter of Melpomene!"

"Whatever are you talking about, Belos? It's your damned literary education again!"

"Her mother, it seems, was a thespian. A mistress of Roscius. She trod the boards. She was of my former profession. An actress, my lord, her mother was an actress!"

"Damn me, Belos, *that* would cause a stir among the turnips if it were known. I fancy they must have been at pains to keep it quiet at Jesmond Place. Folks are so censorious nowadays. There was a time when the daughter of an actress would have been considered an adornment to a gentleman's household, but times, I fear, are changing."

"Who would have thought it of that dry stick, Sir

Antony?" put in Elisabeth. "Tell us, Belos, what happened to the actress?"

"Nobody knows, Miss. She retired from the stage, and nothing more was heard of her. Of course, it is usual to make some sort of financial arrangement; if Lady Jesmond's father was a gentleman, as is so often the case . . ."

"Sir Antony would doubtless wish in any event to make some discreet provision for his wife's mother."

"So we do not know the whereabouts of the lady?"

As a matter of fact, we could take a very good guess. "There is one obvious candidate, don't you agree?" said I, and then as Elisabeth was opening her mouth to utter a name, "but I do not think it can affect recent events, and as the lady presumably wishes to keep her identity a secret, let us assist her to do so. It can do no harm and has no bearing on the present. We have no interest, surely, in exposing a private episode in the past history of the Jesmond family."

"Very well, Ambrose. I think we are of a like mind on this. Belos, you will know of whom we are speaking, perhaps?"

"I have not met any of the parties at Jesmond Place, so I cannot really give an opinion, but there is no need to open old wounds. Let the lady keep her secret. We all have things in our lives which we would not wish to be held up to the light of day."

His face was serious suddenly, and he was looking at his plate as he spoke, as if the mundane pile of chicken bones in front of him were some ancient Roman sacred entrails in which he saw the future. I got us back on to the subject in hand.

"But it certainly casts an interesting light on life at Jesmond Place, does it not?"

"Ambrose, do you think this can be somehow related to the terrible deaths of those two young men?"

I considered carefully, a forkful of tender new peas halfway to my lips. "I do not see why it should be so; after all, it cannot for example affect the legitimacy of the Jesmond marriage or have any bearing on legal matters. But nevertheless, it makes me uneasy, I must confess. The notion that there is one secret buried in that household that has come to light only by chance . . . what else may be hidden there?"

"And what feelings may have been aroused by Sir Antony's second marriage, to the daughter of an actress?" added Elisabeth. "Her parentage might still cause a scandal, were it to become known. You are right about that—let us say nothing on the matter for the present. Ambrose, I am very uneasy for Lady Jesmond's sake. I would like to leave for Jesmond Place straight away. Consider her position, in that house where two sudden deaths have occurred, and her husband does not seem over-affectionate toward her."

I too felt there might be impending danger, that the murderous events at Jesmond Place had not yet run out their course. But I did not wish to expose Elisabeth to them.

"Remember that Dr. Sandys is still there, and a Scottish sawbones of sobriety and good sense may be considered protection against most of the world's evils. Your Lady Jesmond will be quite safe under his guardianship. But Murdoch is not a man of action, I admit. He is not a rash fool-headed hero like myself, and it may be that a man of action is needed on the spot. Very well, I promise you I will betake myself to the Jesmonds' as soon as may be possible. But let us return first to Malfine: I asked Sandys to send a message if there should be any news, by a stable-lad at Jesmond Place to whom I slipped a guinea or two while I was instructing him as to Zaraband's wishes."

"No messenger had arrived before we left. But something may have arrived since then."

Elisabeth and Belos left by coach, to be dragged up Titup Hill and thence over Shotover. I returned to Christ Church to fetch Zaraband and departed from Oxford, rejoicing in the soft warm glow of the afternoon, looking back over a city that floated in the green and misty valley. Before leaving, I had settled my account with Christ Church, for the occupancy of their guest-room and the accommodation of my horse.

In a sense, also, I had settled an account with my younger self.

Part Three

CHAPTER 14

THERE is something about Oxford, lovely though it be, that makes me long for fresh air. The fogs and miasmas of topography and mind give me an irresistible urge to proclaim instant revolution, and in my hot youth I did that very thing, but not in England, where it would have been wasted breath. Here, the servility of the people makes talk of revolution a fantasy.

Yet I shall not succumb to the conventional wisdom that threatens to engulf us: that I and those few survivors of the band who fought with me grow older and wiser. We are simply older, that is all. Within, we are unchanged. Liberty and justice are still worth the fight, against all the dreary weight that this present era brings to press down upon them now that the age of moralizing has begun, and the country is over-run with damned parsons and preachers.

However profound my reflections upon the dullness of the present, I wished to lose no time in getting back to Jesmond Place. Of that I was certain, but I did not wish to return directly to the house itself and confront its master—not yet, at any rate. The landlord of the inn at Combwich had a room, whence I could send over a request to Sandys, asking him to join me without saying anything to the household. The landlord's boy undertook to get this message to him, having been warned that it was for the eyes of the doctor alone.

"Ambrose, I am still most fearful for Lady Jesmond," were Elisabeth's words, when we had returned to Malfine and were seated again on the terrace, as was our wont on these pleasant evenings.

"For her safety in that household?"

"Partly, but there is something beyond that. Jesmond Place is so *enclosed,* so preoccupied are the inhabitants with their own concerns, that somehow the place seems cut off from the real world."

"Yes, I sensed that too. It is more than the mere physical isolation of the house."

"Sir Antony apparently has no interests beyond whatever it is that occupies him in his private quarters; they have no visitors, see nothing of anyone outside. Mrs. Romey was telling me that Sir Antony no longer even cares for anything on the Jesmond estate. I remember her words. 'He used to be dead agin poachers, Sir Antony. When old Cotteslow from Combwich was caught there with his pocket full of rabbits, he went up before Sir Edward Knellys—the coldest devil you ever did see.' Those were her very words. I believe the old man was transported, and it killed him at his age."

Greed blinds some men to everything, as indolence blinds me. For all I know or care, cavalcades of merry poachers may hold pheasant-shooting festivals on the grounds of Malfine.

In the distance, the woods were darkening as dusk descended. Once or twice, the cries of night creatures echoed toward the house. The air was very still. Elisabeth's voice came again through the soft evening.

"Although Lady Jesmond may have something to hide, I cannot believe that she herself is guilty of any crime. I think she would be a victim—not a murderess!"

"From whom is she in danger? Mrs. Romey appears devoted to her mistress. Charnock—we barely know anything of him, but what possible reason could *he* have to murder Clara Jesmond? Assuming that Lady Jesmond would be in danger from the person who has committed the previous murders, I suppose that Charnock might have killed Kelsoe for reasons of his own—say he wanted to replace him in Sir Antony's favor. But why should he have any reason for encompassing the death of Cyriack Jesmond? Charnock would surely have nothing to gain by that. So that leaves Sir Antony, unlikely to have been the killer of his own son, even if for some reason he had disposed of Kelsoe. Do you think Sir Antony could encompass the death of his own wife? Is that what you fear?"

"It is possible, is it not? But somehow, I think we are missing the watchspring in this puzzle. I mean, the mechanism which drives the whole thing forward. What motives lay behind the deaths of Kelsoe and Cyriack Jesmond, think you?"

"In the case of Kelsoe," I returned, "I thought at first it must be a case of murder. But my conversations in Oxford have convinced me that is not necessarily the case—it could, after all, have been suicide. Yet, in the case of Cyriack Jesmond, I cannot believe from all that I know of the young man's character that he also committed suicide. Master Cyriack would never have thought the world a better place without him, nor had such a hopeless opinion of himself and his future in life. And even if he had, even let us suppose him somehow plunged in the depths of despair, why choose such an extraordinary course as placing the prussic acid in his hip-flask and then drinking it down on horseback?"

"So we have one case of possible suicide and one of murder?"

"Yes. But although Cyriack was, I grant you, a most unlovely character, it is hard to see why he should be killed in that deliberate fashion, for poison requires forethought. It is not usually the result of sudden passion—for example, if the late Master Jesmond had provoked tempestuous anger or precipitated an attack by some insulted opponent. I can imagine that he might have died in a duel or a fist-fight, caused by his own hasty temper, but not of slow, planned cunning murder."

She agreed with me, but pointed out that Mrs. Romey had prepared the flask, and might have been motivated by affection for Lady Jesmond.

"Both she and Lady Jesmond might indeed be suspected. We should not lose sight of the possibility, yet we have no evidence on which to act. But it looks black, I must agree."

I should have known what was coming next.

"Ambrose, the blacker it looks for her, the more she needs friends. I am convinced of her innocence and I am persuaded her husband will not take her part. Before the death of his son he seemed utterly preoccupied with some other secret business—some matters concerning that fellow Charnock. He has no time for his wife, that is plain to see."

"Elisabeth, Murdoch Sandys is still there at Jesmond

Place and in any case we have scarcely known the woman for any length of time . . ."

"Dr. Sandys is very well, but he is a prudent man and likely to be too cautious. And besides, he will not have your influence. There is no point in beating about the bush. You are a wealthy aristocrat and he is a poor country doctor. You may command respect: he could only request it, and I somehow do not think it would be accorded him, even if he did intervene on behalf of Lady Jesmond. And who else is there? Oh, Mrs. Romey is devoted enough, but what can she achieve to protect her mistress? There have been two deaths: is not Clara Jesmond the most likely of that household to fall victim if there should be a third?"

"Well . . . I see you cannot abandon your concern for her. Certainly, there have been two deaths in that house—and that is why I cannot allow you to endanger yourself. I shall ride over there in the morning and do what I can for the lady. In any case, I must go and talk to our watchdog Sandys and fetch him back with me to his other patients and his beloved Florence at their charming Lute House. There is probably little more he can do at Jesmond Place. But I insist on one thing—you yourself must not go again to Jesmond Place. It is too dangerous an enterprise."

Elisabeth did not reply. She rose, swinging her skirts, and stepped indoors. Of a lesser woman, it might have been said, she flounced.

CHAPTER 15

I soon found a cause for Cyriack's murder—and one which could have been long festering away. Sandys gave me the news, almost as he shook the summer shower from his cloak in the doorway of the parlor of the Green Lion.

"Ah, Lord Ambrose, I got your message. I agree, it is better for us to have some private conversation here; somehow I have a feeling that at Jesmond Place one is always being overheard—I do not know why. Perhaps it is because that Charnock fellow appears without warning sometimes, or perhaps it is merely because the house is so old that it seems to have a life of its own. Dear me, I grow fanciful!"

"Why, Murdoch Sandys, I had never supposed you so imaginative! But let me call for some ale—or cider. The local perry is excellent, but I do not trust the wine."

A stone flagon of their perry arrived, and Sandys took a deep pull.

"Ah, my mouth was dry!"

It was necessary to broach a rather delicate subject: that

his scientific superiors in chemistry considered that it was quite possible, in some cases, for a person to survive long enough after taking prussic acid to perform a few actions such as re-corking the poison bottle. To my relief, Sandys took it with great generosity of spirit.

"Well, I am but a country physician with no time to experiment. If that is what Professor Daubeny says, then I will most happily accept it and be overruled. People imagine that any scientific statement must be an absolute law, but it depends entirely on the state of knowledge of the person who makes it. Let us therefore imagine that it was possible that John Kelsoe committed suicide—but we still have the cause of his wretchedness to discover, do we not?"

I assented, and Sandys continued, "Lord Ambrose, I have been talking to the housekeeper, Mrs. Romey. She let slip that there is a good reason, after all, for her ladyship to wish Master Cyriack off the face of the earth. After her husband's death, any relationship with another man would mean the possible loss of all her inheritance; Cyriack would have gained everything. She and her stepson must have been mortal enemies the moment that infamous will was signed. If he could prove her guilty of some illicit connection, she would forfeit all claims over the estate and her stepson would immediately come into his own. No money need be spared from the Jesmond estate for the provision of his stepmother. He would enjoy all the revenues—every penny. She might have wished to ensure her stepson could not curtail her pleasures when she became a widow!"

"Yes," I agreed, "and Cyriack's violent behavior toward her was another good reason why she should want him dead, for what sort of treatment might she not have to bear after Sir Antony's death? It might be that she has more to gain than anyone by Cyriack's demise. And after all, who else would have an interest in poisoning Cyriack?"

"Not his father, who is plainly shattered with grief!"

"It is a most extraordinary business. And have you discovered what Charnock is doing in that household?"

"No, but I can tell you one thing."

Murdoch Sandys leaned forward across the scrubbed wooden table of the inn parlor.

"It happens at night!"

Before he could say more on the subject of Charnock, there was a sudden interruption. The landlord's wife Naomi burst into the parlor, her face flushed with excitement.

"Oh gentlemen, here's news! Do you know who has just ridden past? He must be making for Jesmond, for there's nothing else in that direction except the moor!"

I had indeed registered the sound of horses clipping past the parlor window, and the shadow that fell briefly across the light.

"Who was it? I did not see the coach."

"Sir Edward Knellys!" She added, in a whisper: "He's the Justice of the Peace!"

Sandys said fiercely, "Knellys is no fool, I've heard. But he's said to be the most unmerciful of men!"

The landlady clasped her hands to her throat. It was like some instinctive protective gesture.

In spite of all I had said to Elisabeth, I began to fear for that fading blonde beauty at Jesmond Place, with her distracted husband and the mysterious weakling Charnock as her principal companions and defenders.

"I think we should follow Sir Edward, and see what he requires of Sir Antony and his lady."

It was a short ride to Jesmond Place, and I held Zaraband

in check. I did not want us to overtake Sir Edward, in case he would not disclose his purpose fully in front of strangers. And I was fairly certain what that purpose might be.

The house, with its blackened beams and stained yellow stonework, seemed to loom up as we approached; the jutting little mullioned windows appeared made for retaining secrets rather than for letting in the honest light of day. I detest a dark house. Even in summer, Jesmond Place had a disturbing air—as of something old and decayed that has endured beyond its natural span.

I could see a carriage standing before the entrance, and a liveried coachman gazing impassively into space—clearly, the visitor had just arrived. Suddenly, from within the house came a long, piercing cry, a wail that echoed despairingly to the outer world, as if the mere appearance of the visitor engendered fear.

Dashing up the steps, we entered the hall. A tall, cadaverous man, whom I conjectured to be Sir Edward Knellys, stood within. He had a distinctive big jaw, and an unpleasant mouthful of bulldog teeth. Facing him, at the top of the stairs, was Lady Jesmond, who seemed almost fainting with fright. She was leaning against the stair-post, and behind her in the shadows stood the housekeeper.

Clara Jesmond had one hand to her mouth, and the other was tearing frantically at her own hair, the long fair hair that hung down over her back and naked shoulders; she was wearing a white silk bedgown, crumpled from her sleep. It was apparent that she had just emerged from her room and had not stopped to throw on a cloak or robe.

As we watched, it was impossible not to wince, such was the pain she must be inflicting on herself as her long fingers pulled and twisted amidst her tangled locks, her diamond ring flashing in the few rays of sun that penetrated through a window on the upper landing.

Suddenly, we were aware the agitated movement had stopped. Mrs. Romey had emerged from the shadows and taken hold of her ladyship's hand, which she held now in her own, crooning gently as if to a child.

"There, my pet, my honey. There, nothing can get ye."

Sir Antony was already in the hall, "Knellys, what is the meaning of this?"

"I have a duty to perform, Jesmond—you must know that. From information that has been laid—"

"That old devil of a lawyer!" Mrs. Romey's voice rang out in indignation, and I was reminded of her former career as an actress. "Candless has been to see you, Sir Edward, I'll be bound! Stirring up trouble with lies and falsehoods!"

Knellys ignored this outburst. His voice was low, unforced, yet as cold as ice.

"Sir Antony, the information against your wife is of the gravest kind. I have a warrant to take her up on the most serious of charges."

"What is it?"

Sir Antony's voice was dry, brusque. No instant defense of his wife, no springing to assist her at this terrible moment.

Knellys' voice said the word we were all expecting to hear, yet one can seldom believe one's ears when that word is uttered. It came like freezing cold on the north wind, and echoed in a chilling gust through the dark hallway.

"Murder. The murder of Cyriack Jesmond."

Lady Jesmond seemed to be whimpering, rather than weeping. There was the sound of her sobbing breath, and nothing else, for a few moments.

Knellys moved forward, his long figure outlined against

the light of the open doorway. "Clara Annabelle Jesmond, you are hereby charged with the murder of Cyriack Douglas Antony Jesmond, that on the twenty-third day of May in the year of our lord eighteen hundred and thirty-three you did encompass his death."

There was a long pause. Sir Edward was staring at Lady Jesmond, and in his face there was almost a touch of fear. The last word he spoke was uttered in a whisper.

"And, madam, think yourself fortunate you are not charged with *witchcraft*!"

At this, even Sir Antony seemed to recoil in horror.

"Witchcraft, Knellys? How can you bring such a charge against my wife?"

And Sandys, behind me, starting forward: "Aye, man, 'tis barbaric! D'ye believe in witches in these parts still, ye poor fools?"

Knellys was as cold as the grave and cut through their protests. "I have evidence, gentlemen, else I should not act in this fashion. Things have been brought into this house that can only serve for terrible purposes; whether for science or for witchcraft, they have accomplished certain death. And who, besides Lady Clara Jesmond, would profit by the decease of the heir? Madam, I must ask you to accompany me."

A fearful picture rose up in my mind, of Clara Jesmond thrown into prison, into a filthy stinking cell shared with the mad, the sick and the villainous. And then a worse one, of Clara Jesmond at the scaffold with a rope around her neck and her hands pinioned behind her.

I stepped forward from the shadows in the hallway. Knellys, I think, had not realized that I was present at all.

"Ambrose Malfine, at your service, Sir Edward. You will, I believe, have heard of me. Let me remind you that the law of this country has not recognized witchcraft as a crime for nearly a hundred years, and if you believe in such rubbish, it is all the more to your discredit. If the charge is that of murder, are you truly determined to remove Lady Jesmond to prison? What is this evidence of which you speak?"

Knellys seemed astonished at this apparition. Clearly, whatever he had planned for this scene, he did not expect the presence of a stranger who might stand between him and the arrest of Clara Jesmond. Especially not a stranger of wealth and status. Most especially not a damned tricky radical with no respect for legal pipsqueaks.

"Yes, of course, the whole county knows of you, Lord Ambrose."

There was no need to say more, but he did. People always do.

"I understand that you have been instrumental on a previous occasion in helping an accused man cheat the gallows."

"Cheat, Sir Edward? If you refer to the affair of the gypsy who was accused of the murders at Crawshay's farm, that man was innocent! But at least there seemed to be some real evidence against him—"

"The law does not require me to disclose the evidence which I have against Lady Jesmond. Not yet, and not to you. I have the powers of Coroner and Justice. Inquests will be held on these two unfortunate men, but there is suspicion enough upon this woman to already implicate her in the second death. You, Lord Ambrose, are not a lawyer, nor do you have any official role in these proceedings. I must ask you to step aside. This woman is under arrest."

But I moved forward as he did, and blocked him.

"You would be unwise to try to resolve this matter with force, Sir Edward, upon this occasion. No doubt you expected that in this house there would be no one to resist your removal of Lady Jesmond. Her husband appears disinclined to make a gallant stand in her favor—you must have been pretty sure of that in advance, or else you would have brought a couple of men with you. Sir Antony does not seem likely to defend his wife—at all events, he is shrinking back at this very moment."

Here there was an uncomfortable shuffling as Sir Antony, thus detected in the act of slipping backward, safely away from any possible conflict, became aware that eyes were turning to him. Behind him, there was a kind of scuttling up the stairs. Unimpeded, Charnock was making good his escape.

"But here am I, Sir Edward, I stand here, and I desire you to reconsider. Be reasonable, man. Do not take her ladyship straight away—allow her to remain here, confined to her room, until you have made further scrutiny of this 'evidence.' "

I moved a little closer to Sir Edward, and tall though he was, I towered above him. My damned long shanks!

"Malfine, you have no right—"

"None whatever, Sir Edward. Nor do I claim one. I merely ask a favor of you. There would be nothing contrary to law in this—house arrest is a perfectly well-known procedure. Let Lady Jesmond remain here on that basis."

Still, he seemed inclined to dispute.

"How do I know she will not pursue her damned devices if she is left here?"

Murdoch Sandys now played his part in our little drama.

"Sir Edward, I am a medical man, and surely you may regard me as being independent in this matter—I barely know any members of this household. Would you not allow me to consider any evidence you may have from a professional viewpoint, before you take Lady Jesmond from her home?"

And here the good doctor introduced a delicate tact, which I must confess was at that moment beyond me.

"After all, Sir Edward, you are an educated man. You will not yourself believe in this village gossip, these tales of witchcraft. I am sure you take an interest in scientific matters, a man of such wide learning as yourself! I believe you to be a rational man, sir, and not in thrall to country superstitions."

He took the bait, of course. Flattery is a sure snare. I have fallen for it myself many a time, with women.

As he left, I caught up with him in one or two strides.

"Malfine?"

"These charges against Clara Jesmond, what possible evidence can you have? Witchcraft! Such matters are for village gossips and country parsons."

Knellys seemed reluctant to answer me, but drawled out a reply, from the side of his mouth, as it were. It seemed an unpleasant habit with him never to speak straight to your face.

"No, Malfine, of course I have no belief in witchcraft! And yet there are witnesses who can give evidence of strange occurrences here—flames seen leaping from the chimneys at night, and cartloads of goods brought from the town which I made it my business to examine."

"What sort of goods?"

"Some quite ordinary, such as coals, yet even when summer is almost here, brought in quantities. Some most strange: lumps of glass, small flasks of powder and liquids."

"But why connect them with Lady Jesmond?"

"These things are brought here—and young Cyriack dies. Surely we must suspect poison, or some devious attempt upon his life which succeeded, by whatever means. This cannot be an accident and the first question to ask is, who would benefit by his death? Why, his stepmother, Lady Jesmond! The whole district knows that there was no love lost between them! Besides, there have been two deaths here."

"But why should Clara Jesmond have murdered young Kelsoe?"

He laughed abruptly and climbed into his coach.

"Haven't you figured it out? I have. She had the best of reasons, Malfine. And I don't mean love!" Incomprehensible then, but the meaning of this remark would become apparent.

He turned his head away, slammed the carriage door and the waiting coachman cracked his whip.

"I am sure that she is not guilty of murder, Lord Ambrose," said Sandys, as I turned back into the house, "but Knellys seems to me implacable. He will not allow her to remain at liberty for long, especially not if there is some outcry against her. What was that accusation? Not merely murder, but—"

"Witchcraft! What an absurdity! Yet there is no doubt there are many in the countryside who still believe in such powers, in foretelling the future and casting spells and the like. Lord knows, I encountered old medicinal remedies—some kill, some cure—when my wounds were healing. What was it Cyriack said—about seeing smoke from the chimney? That was odd, was it not?"

"Yes, I suppose it was. I do not think any fires had been lit. The weather was quite warm."

I was silent for a few minutes. The scrap of paper which Elisabeth had found in Kelsoe's room came into my mind. What had it said?

Coals of fire.
Quicksilver.
Cakes of glass.

Coals of fire might certainly relate to the smoking chimney which Cyriack had seen, presumably as he rode toward the house in the early hours of that May morning. But what of the other things, the quicksilver and the cakes of glass? "Lumps of glass"—had not Sir Edward Knellys claimed these were among the mysterious contents of the cartloads brought to Jesmond Place? Evidently there had been more than the one of which I had heard at the Green Lion. Were these the ingredients for a witch's potion? Perhaps Clara Jesmond was intending to add "eye of newt and toe of frog" to them, and bubble it all up in some noisome cauldron.

"And she committed murder by magic?" My question was rhetorical. "That seems to be what Knellys believes. That Clara Jesmond killed Cyriack with one baleful curse or spell, knocked him clean off his horse with her black arts. There is the solid scientific evidence of prussic acid in his hip-flask, which Daubeny found in his experiment in Oxford."

"I do not think Knellys himself would believe in witchcraft. He is an educated man, not a country bumpkin. It's time we talked to Lady Jesmond herself."

And I agreed. "Tell me, Sandys, did you learn anything useful while I was away?"

"There is nothing I can particularly describe, my lord, yet this household is not one I care for."

"Everyone here seems to have their own secretive life," I concurred. "Belos has learned that Mrs. Romey was an actress at some time in the past—and may still be, for all we know, though it seems she left the stage many years ago."

"That would certainly account for some things about her," said Sandys. "Her speech, for instance, which is not always that of the ordinary countrywoman."

"Very true. But if she wishes to keep her theatrical life a secret, why, I see no reason to disoblige her. It was all long ago and seems to have little bearing on the present."

"I quite agree," said Sandys. "Sir Antony might not care it to be known that he had a former actress in his employ. It would be unkind if Mrs. Romey were to lose her place."

"Very well, we'll say nothing for the present. But there is one person of whom we might make some inquiries—the clergyman at Cyriack's funeral service. A parson is supposed to know something of the local activities, and to meddle away, keeping an eye on his flock and so forth."

"He was from Otterhampton, which I believe is the next village to Combwich. Less than half an hour's ride, I would estimate."

It was about a quarter, on Zaraband, even allowing for an uphill stretch at the end. On the other side of the hill was a small tower of rough stone, which when we descended toward it proved to be that of a tiny church, sleeping like a mouse in the sun. A huge yew stood in the churchyard, which was overgrown, rich in wild flowers, overhung with trees. I stepped onto the cool porch, looked up, and saw a martin's nest in the roof.

The door was locked. The lock looked ancient, a huge iron affair that had probably deterred generations of would-be worshippers and plain nosy-parkers, and would still not yield an inch.

The place was not quite deserted. As I turned back toward the lane that ran alongside the church, there was a movement round the other side of the churchyard; I moved swiftly toward it and through a gap in the hedge came pushing a small family of sheep, placidly clipping the long grass. Nature appeared to be landscaping after its own fashion. I thought of the story of the rector who had kept his horses here.

There was a house behind the church that was like to be the rectory, where I thought I might find the young curate or his master the rector, but like the church it was all locked up, silent, deserted. Absenteeism reigned in Otterhampton.

CHAPTER 16

CLARA Jesmond's room was a large oak-beamed chamber, where some recent attempt had been made to lighten the effect of the wooden paneling by giving it a wash of pale paint. But the room seemed dark and stuffy: the furniture was evidently a legacy of the past, heavy stuff, with a great black-posted bed, and a massive armchair with carved feet, like those of some big animal. Over the fireplace hung the portrait of some previous mistress of the house: a thin severe face, floating palely above the gray ruches and drapery of her dress. Hardly the picture for the bedroom of a nervous young wife, but no doubt it was some aristocratic ancestress of the Jesmonds.

Perched among these deadweights of the Jesmond family history were some trifling possessions which must have been the present lady's own choice—little gilt-framed pictures—a child with a kitten, a weeping nymph—that sort of thing. My eye fell on a flowery vase of pink and gold china, fighting a despairing battle for cheerfulness in the midst of weighty gloom.

Although the day promised to be comparatively warm, the nominal mistress of the house was curled up in the armchair wearing a wrapper of pale blue wool and with a rug over her knees. Standing by her side was Mrs. Romey, holding out a cup.

"I was just trying to get my lady to drink some warm milk," said she. She put the cup down.

Clara Jesmond spoke to Sandys immediately.

"Dr. Sandys, my health is not good. I have quite lost my appetite."

This, murmured in an undertone from the invalid in the chair, was an understatement. Sandys afterward told me that he had observed her carefully during his stay beneath her husband's roof, and at any sound, at the creaking of a door or the distant barking of a dog, she would start from her chair with such alarm that he could observe the very pulse beating at her throat. The food on her plate was barely touched: her clothes had begun to hang loosely about that once-plump form. And I observed for myself the great dark hollows that lay under her eyes, making her look almost an old woman. The sight seemed to recall something to me—what exactly, I could not tell.

Sandys came directly to the point. "Lady Jesmond, you will be aware that there is but one likely explanation of the deaths of those two unfortunate young men."

She answered him, but she was looking up at me, straight into my face; her lips were murmuring so that I saw rather than heard the word being formed.

"Poison."

I nodded. "And prussic acid in all probability. Fast-acting and without remedy."

The head, with its weight of pretty blonde hair, nodded.

"The most alarming aspect is that there appears to be no connection between the deaths of Mr. Cyriack Jesmond and young Dr. Kelsoe," Sandys continued. "It seems we must dismiss the possibility of an accident which could have overtaken them both. Can you think of any possible reason why anyone should have some malicious intent toward both of them?"

"No, Dr. Sandys, none whatever. I have racked my brains to find one, but it seems quite impossible, does it not? Cyriack was—well, he was a rash young man sometimes, but he was my husband's only son and heir, and as for Dr. Kelsoe, I believe he was scarcely known at all here. There can have been no reason whatsoever for anyone at Jesmond Place to wish poor Dr. Kelsoe in his grave."

Tears stood in her eyes. I said nothing, and let Sandys continue.

"Your ladyship, we must then face a terrible possibility. This is not the work of someone who has murdered for a rational purpose—this is the work of a lunatic, one who kills for the pleasure of it. And that means that anyone may be a victim."

She was shrinking back into the chair, her face very white. The housekeeper made a sound of alarm and bent down to arrange a shawl round her mistress's shoulders.

"You're frightening my lady, doctor, with your wild ideas!"

"No, no," murmured Lady Jesmond. "We must think about it. But what are we to do?"

I now took a part in the proceedings. "Lady Jesmond, I would urge that you and your housekeeper both take your meals here in your room, and that you eat only food and drink prepared by Mrs. Romey. Do not touch anything else—even if it is only a dish of tea."

"But how long is this to continue, Lord Ambrose? I cannot remain like that indefinitely! And Sir Edward Knellys wants to take me away—"

Sandys answered for me.

"Lady Jesmond, I believe it to be the case that these are the acts of a deranged mind, which is very close to the edge when it commences its terrible machinations, and that soon it will break down altogether. You will be exonerated, most certainly. Be patient, I beg you, and follow my advice!"

She nodded, mopping her eyes, and we left her. I realized that for much of the time while we had been talking, Mrs. Romey had been sipping at the cup which her mistress had refused. A betrayingly intimate action.

"I think I have heard her weeping at night," said Sandys, as we descended the stairs, "though the house has some odd properties; because of the twisting staircases and odd little rooms leading hither and thither, it is often difficult to tell where any sound is coming from. At first I thought that I should be put in the attic story, where young Kelsoe had perished, but Sir Antony desired me to remain near his wife's chamber, in case she should need medical assistance. He seemed to mention this to me in a rather desultory way, as if he were more preoccupied with something that was going on elsewhere, but this is a frequent occurrence with him. He said that Mrs. Romey had been sleeping in his wife's chamber, but that he had put a stop to it. He wanted Lady Jesmond to have a proper physician nearby, but that, I think, was an excuse. He does not like the housekeeper being so near her."

"Does Charnock have any medical skill?"

"None, it appears. I cannot account for his presence here, but Sir Antony has said that he assists him with his work—whatever that may be. He has no medical duties."

"Well, that scarcely throws any light on that curious creature. What happened at young Cyriack's funeral, by the way? There seems no end to the descriptions of obsequies I am obliged to endure!"

CHAPTER 17

BUT he was a good observer, Sandys, and gave me a precise account of Cyriack's funeral. It had been very different from that of Kelsoe. There, few mourners were present, though those few were sincerely afflicted by the loss of a modest and promising young man. For the funeral of Cyriack Jesmond the small church of St. Chad's was nigh packed out with local people, yet Sandys did not have any feeling that they were mourning their young squire, but rather that their faces were impassive, guarding their feelings for the occasion, and they had mainly come because they were Jesmond tenants and fearful not to make the right show. Of course, the rector, who deemed the occasion worthy of his attendance, said the appropriate words, but somehow, said Sandys, they did not carry much conviction.

There they were, huddled in the church, the family in the front pew and the rustics at the back. I pictured the scene. A clammy day, said Sandys, a kind of damp miasma arising on the moor outside, and the faces within mostly pale and drawn or quite blank and unreadable. As he spoke (I should have used the word "droned"), Sandys surveyed the mourners.

Lady Jesmond was seated between Mr. Charnock and Sir Antony; she had scarcely been able to enter the church unassisted. She was wearing mourning now, a full black gown which seemed to drag her down. As she entered on the arm of Sir Antony, with Mrs. Romey, the housekeeper, supporting her on the other side, one or two voices were heard murmuring in sympathy.

"I do think there'll be a third burying before summer come." That was one voice, and a soft sighing of agreement rippled along the hard wooden pews at the back of the little church.

Sandys followed this sad trio of the Jesmonds and their housekeeper into the church and expected them to be seated thus together, as they had entered. But Sir Antony did an unkind thing—even cruel, considering the state of his wife's health. His words rang through the church. "Charnock, take her other side! Mrs. Romey, you will leave off helping her."

With a shock, Sandys saw that the fellow, who had lagged behind, went past and, without a word, obeyed his master, though it seems that he flinched, like a dog reluctantly carrying out a disagreeable order which might be reinforced with a blow. There was an open stare of shock on Mrs. Romey's face, and Sandys thought for a moment that she would refuse to leave her mistress, but she reluctantly gave way, and the lady was assisted, half-fainting, into the family pew.

The housekeeper took her place behind, with the few other servants—the Jesmonds' coachman and a couple of maids—who also attended the last rites of their young squire. Sir Antony had made her inferior status very plain.

For Sandys' part, he did not venture to enter the same pew as the Jesmonds, and observing empty seats on the other side of the church, took himself thither. There, he told me, he observed that Sir Antony's face bore the signs of real grief. There were tears in his eyes as the prayers were said over the coffined body of his only son. Charnock looked merely bewildered, as if trying to make some sense of the situation in which he found himself. Behind, the servants were impassive. Mrs. Romey in particular had recovered herself and was staring straight ahead, her back upright. "She has a handsome face, a large and brilliant eye, a fine wide brow—a face that made me pause, I knew not why, but it is all of a piece with what you surmised of her past history," added the doctor.

As for Lady Jesmond, Sandys thought that the sight of the coffin might undo her altogether, and that a fit of hysteria or fainting might follow, so he held himself in readiness to offer medical assistance. Yet, strange to say, she seemed unchanged as the pallbearers solemnly moved down the church to set their black-draped burden before the altar. She became perhaps even a little calmer as the service progressed.

At the end, however, Sir Antony was forced to leave his lady in the charge of the housekeeper, for the traditional usage was followed and only the men went to the graveside. It was at this point that Sandys, following the other men, became aware that another gentleman had joined them in the church; he presumably had been sitting behind him during the service. He was a respectable-looking fellow, a little stout, in a suit of good black cloth, and stood back as Sir Antony approached the grave. Not a member of the family,

Murdoch Sandys concluded; nor did he have the air of being a local country gentleman nor yet a servant.

Sir Antony showed far more feeling than expected. His sobs were unrestrained as the wet clods descended with dull thuds upon his only son's coffin.

"Ah, Dr. Sandys, I have much to grieve for," he suddenly broke out, as the drizzling rain washed thin mud over the varnished wood of the coffin; it disappeared at last under the spadefuls of earth that the gravediggers were tipping in, and Sir Antony finally consented to go indoors. Charnock had stood nervously at the back all the while, offering no assistance to his master.

There was no hospitable ceremony of funeral baked meats, as had been held for Kelsoe; the master and mistress of the house were not able to sustain the niceties of such an occasion, their grief being now too close to home. Sir Antony and Lady Jesmond went immediately to their separate rooms. As he mounted the stairs, Sir Antony called out, "Mrs. Romey, would you please have something to eat sent up to Mr. Charnock's room. There is some work I wish him to undertake immediately. I do not myself want anything, but Mr. Candless and I have a matter to discuss. Mr. Candless, what will you take?"

The stout party whom Sandys had observed at the graveside appeared behind us in the hallway. "No, thank you, Sir Antony, I won't take anything just now. I have brought the papers with me." They vanished into the dining room.

That was as much as Sandys was able to tell me, but that evening I learned more. There seemed no likelihood of a normal dinner being served in this turbulent household, and I went into the dining room in search of fodder only to find Lady Jesmond getting up from the table, an empty plate before her. Sandys was there already, urging her to try something. "Do you have something light, Mrs. Romey? A little neat's-foot jelly, perhaps, or some fish?"

"No, nothing for me, Romey," said her ladyship. "Perhaps a dish of tea—no more."

Mrs. Romey turned to me.

"Lord Ambrose, Dr. Sandys, no doubt you would like something to eat, but there is nothing prepared. The kitchenmaids have not come up from the village—I do not think they will come to this house again, to tell the truth, and I have been looking after my mistress. I can have some bread and ham sent through—or a dish of eggs, if you would prefer."

"Thank you, Mrs. Romey, I would like something." I glanced across at Sandys. "But we shan't trouble anyone to bring it to us—we will happily join you at your table, if you are having something. I do not stand upon ceremony myself."

Sandys nodded agreement, and this brought a smile from the housekeeper. "Well, Sir Antony would not like gentlemen under his roof to eat with a servant, but perhaps on this occasion, since the circumstances are very unusual . . ."

"Oh, they are, Mrs. Romey, are they not? Most unusual."

We followed her into a neat room, the housekeeper's parlor, plainly and solidly furnished. She disappeared into the cavernous kitchen, and produced a tray with a rabbit pie with country pastry and thick wine gravy, but it was served with some care at a table covered with a white linen cloth. Mrs. Romey wiped her mouth delicately with a napkin and rose to fetch a decanter from the small black-oak sideboard.

"Will you take a glass of Madeira, gentlemen? It is perhaps a little early in the day, but the church was chilling."

This seemed an agreeable idea. And perhaps it would induce Mrs. Romey to unleash a few secrets.

She raised the glass to her eyes, regarding the rich color of the wine, and made a few comments of the kind one might expect—what a sad occasion, how young was the poor gentleman, and so forth.

"Mrs. Romey, I am a plain Scot," said Sandys. "I cannot sing any false praises of Mr. Cyriack Jesmond, since I knew nothing of him or his qualities. But let us be clear here: from what I *do* know of him, he seems no great loss to the world. Sir Antony grieves, that is true, but he is, I think, the only one truly distressed. Forgive me, but I do not care for hypocrisy. What did you think of Cyriack Jesmond?"

There was a long pause and I thought she would refuse to answer him. Then she got up, walked across the room, and suddenly pulled the door open wide. There was no one in the passageway beyond.

Returning to her seat, she did not close the door, but was watchful. What a household, where even the housekeeper fears spies!

"This is a very unhappy house, sir," she began. "Lady Jesmond is not at all well—perhaps you would watch over her, Doctor?" She hesitated and then plunged on, twisting her napkin between her fingers. "Her health is very poor at present. She seems unable to get any rest, and Sir Antony does not like me to be close to her."

I had observed this for myself.

"Why, Mrs. Romey? Why does he keep you away from her?"

She dropped her handsome head suddenly, staring down at the white surface of the table. "He wanted . . . wants . . . no one else to be near her." There was a long pause.

I think she would have spoken more.

But there were footsteps.

Charnock's thin black shape came into view at the end of the passageway.

"Ah, Dr. Sandys—and Lord Ambrose! Sir Antony desired me to ask . . . but I see you have had something to eat. Well, it is no matter, then."

His eyes swept round the housekeeper's room. Mrs. Romey stood up, once more with that expression of cold restraint I had witnessed in the church. She said nothing, and as the silence lengthened it became apparent that Charnock had nothing more to say, but would not leave. Was he under instructions not to allow us to have a private conversation with the housekeeper? Perhaps, unseen, he had followed us as we left the dining room and reported back to his master. He was tugging nervously at his cravat.

There seemed no further prospect of gleaning anything from the housekeeper on that occasion. We stood up, thanked her and followed Charnock down the passageway.

Yet we had learned something.

It was not so very odd that both Sir Antony and Mrs. Romey should desire Sandys to watch over her ladyship. But it was odd that they seemed so highly suspicious of one another.

I had already made up my mind to make a few inquiries of Mr. Candless, but as it happened I had no need. I wanted to speak further to Mrs. Romey. It seemed she might hold the key to a great many secrets in this house.

It was a fine evening, however, and I took Zaraband out for a gallop across the moor. It was light still, though the stars were visible already, and small moths and night insects flitted through the air. The Arab flew across the grass and scrubby heather as if she would carry me into another world, but as we turned back reluctantly to Jesmond Place, I saw its muddled and twisted chimneys sticking up into the sky. The real world indeed! And a dangerous one. I thought with relief of Elisabeth, safe in the cool marble expanses of Malfine.

Back at Jesmond Place, all seemed quiet, and I determined to have further talk with Mrs. Romey. I therefore descended the stairs to the housekeeper's quarters. There was not a soul about—nor even a sound, save the occasional creak of some old beam in the depths of the building. From somewhere above came an occasional noise, which I identified after a few moments' thought. It was the chinking of glass—not the sort that a bottle makes against the rim of a tumbler, but something much more sharp and careful.

I forgot all about the sound, however, as I entered the realm of the kitchen, for as I identified a larder, and to give my mission some pretext, helped myself to a plate from a stack on the dresser, Mrs. Romey herself entered.

"Can I get you something, my lord?"

"Oh yes, thank you, Mrs. Romey. Is there some cold meat or cheese—something of that sort?"

The last thing I desired, in truth, was some thick mouthfuls of cold rustic collop, doubtless served with no herbs or sauce, but it was too late to wish I had thought of a better request.

Mrs. Romey sallied into the larder and emerged with a great serving-dish, which she set on the table. She then took up a sharp carving-knife and began to cut into the meat. "Pressed brisket of beef," she explained to my reluctant visage, then lit a couple of candles and laid a place for me at the great scrubbed table.

To my surprise, the plain-looking beef had a better taste than I had expected. "Peppercorns, bayleaf, thyme, and I add a glass or two of white wine to the stock," said Mrs. Romey after a few minutes, observing my gesture of appreciation. Evidently the former actress had learned to cook.

"Mrs. Romey, we were having a conversation earlier on which was . . . interrupted."

That was the best term I could find to describe Charnock's abrupt incursion earlier on, when we had probably been on the point of learning something germane.

The housekeeper was clearing away my plate; now she brought out something else from the larder. It was a china mold covered with a plate, and she proceeded to turn out a quivering translucence of a rich wine color. "Claret jelly," she said, and laid a silver spoon and a small jug of thick cream in front of me.

"You have added a little something to this . . ." I hazarded a guess. "Good cooks always do."

She beamed. "Some raspberry preserve. Oh, and the juice of a lemon, just to sharpen it up a little."

"Of course! How inspired!"

"You must try my Dutch flummery sometime."

"Er, yes."

I'm sure it was delicious, whatever it might have been. But now I had to get her off the subject.

"Mrs. Romey, now that Master Cyriack Jesmond is dead—"

She was turning away from the table, but swung back suddenly, and took up my sentence as if I had intended it to mean that Cyriack's death was a blessing, which perhaps it might have been. "But it was little comfort to see Candless in the church, that I can tell you, Lord Ambrose," she confided.

"Who is he? He has the air of a lawyer."

"You are right enough. He is Sir Antony's man of business, come from Bristol, I suppose, to make ready a new will."

"In connection with the death of Master Cyriack Jesmond? Under the old will he would have been the heir, presumably, after her ladyship's lifetime?"

That was the usual arrangement. The widow would enjoy the estate and its income until her death and then it would pass to the eldest son. Lady Jesmond, of course, was Cyriack's stepmother, but that would presumably have made no difference to the legal arrangements.

To my surprise, the housekeeper seemed suddenly to be boiling with rage.

"Yes, my lord, that is the usual arrangement, I believe, but, curse Sir Antony's heart and eyes, something else was intended here! When Sir Antony died, her ladyship was only to have an income from the estate as long as she did not—"

"Did not remarry? But that is a usual provision, is it not? Perhaps somewhat mean-spirited, but not uncommon."

"Not only that. If she was to . . . to engage in . . . I believe the words are 'to engage in any illicit connection'!"

"If she were to have a lover—is that it?"

"Yes. I did not want to say it, but that's what it meant. Anyway, if that were to happen, the whole thing would go immediately to Cyriack—to that creature, who wasn't fit to wipe her ladyship's shoes! And she would not get another penny!"

"The will spelled that out? But, surely, there was no danger. All she had to do was to maintain a spotless reputation," I said quietly.

"Yes, and she is the most innocent lamb that ever walked!

But even putting something like that in the will, you see, and making it known—why, that would make people think! It would make them look out for anything—any small thing that might suggest she's guilty. You know what folk are! That was the will Candless drew up for Sir Antony but ten days ago—and he signed it and crowed about it to the mistress!"

The housekeeper had fine eyes, deep and lustrous, but they were brimming now with indignant tears.

What she said about the potential scandal of such a will was true enough. In a small country community, there was no need for an actual open accusation of infidelity. The meaning of Knellys' comment, that Clara had the best of reasons for killing Kelsoe, suddenly became apparent. The young man might have compromised her hopes of inheritance, and no doubt Candless had talked to his friend, Knellys, of the Jesmond family testament. An unusual provision in the will, an explicit mention of the possibility—that would set the tongues clacking. Why, the gossips would say, had Sir Antony seen fit to make such a condition at all, unless he had grounds to suspect that his widow might dishonor his memory? The provision in the will was practically a guarantee of notoriety.

Had there been anything about Lady Jesmond's conduct to have provoked this piece of cruelty? It was possible that Sir Antony was an elderly household tyrant, an aged British Othello, eaten up with groundless suspicions of a young and still-beautiful wife. Why will old men marry lovely young women if they then spend the rest of their days in an agony of distrust?

I pondered also upon the curious fact that Sir Antony had made this proviso known. Usually old men who feared betrayal were desperately anxious to cover up the fact. "There's no fool like an old fool" is a harsh saying, yet a common one. Indeed, Cyriack himself had used it to Lady Jesmond after Kelsoe's funeral. But perhaps Sir Antony had suspected his wife of something, and wanted to bring pressure to bear upon her behavior, and this may have been a means of warning her.

I tried to console the woman. "Well, it's all over now, for young Cyriack lies in the churchyard yonder. Sir Antony will have to make a new will, and I suppose your mistress may yet have children, in any case?"

The housekeeper gave a short and bitter laugh. "No chance of that, Doctor. Sir Antony will keep to his own room! He cannot do the business, excuse me, my lord, as the old country people say. No," said Mrs. Romey, "there'll be no son to follow him now. He has a cousin in Virginia—that's the nearest heir."

"But he'll have to make *some* allowance for your mistress. And surely he will make a new will after Cyriack's death?"

"Oh aye, there'll be some provision to keep her body and soul together, I suppose. But I pray there's no lying rubbish in it to shame her, like the last time!"

The housekeeper sat down for a few minutes, and her indignation gradually subsided. She rose, resuming a more suitable impassivity, and turned as if to leave the room, but then seemed to remember her duties.

"Do you want anything else, my lord? There's a nice piece of Cheddar cheese. I could toast a couple of slices for you in a chafing-dish, with a little ale and butter?"

"No, thank you, Mrs. Romey." Though somehow I was developing an appetite for these country dishes. Another evening, perhaps, I might ask for cheese cooked in a silver chafing-dish in the old-fashioned way. Yes, upon reflection, it seemed rather appetizing.

But Mrs. Romey had left the room and my mind was occupied with the strange course of events. How did such a testament fit into the drama that had been unfolding beneath this roof? Had Sir Antony suspected his wife of infidelity at the time it was signed, ten days previously?

Was there something which might have been connected with the sequence of murderous events in this household?

The will had been signed just before the death of young Kelsoe.

CHAPTER 18

LADY Jesmond looked up from the depths of her armchair. I had knocked on the door of her room, and been admitted, to find Sandys already there.

"Ah, Malfine, I was just taking her ladyship's pulse. Madam, you must not allow yourself to become excited."

For Clara Jesmond was already looking flustered and her agitation increased at my next words. "Now, madam, I have spoken to Mrs. Romey and she has told me about the will your husband had made. I will not go into the distressing details of the provisions of that document, but you must tell us the truth of the matter; it is very probably, though I admit not certainly, the best way out of the situation in which you find yourself. What happened here? I suggest we begin with the arrival in this house of Dr. John Kelsoe."

She had stopped weeping. Perhaps, I thought, with a touch of my usual cynicism, perhaps the real desperation of her situation had come home, and she knew that there were no subterfuges left.

"Very well, Lord Ambrose. The first thing is, that I do not know why Dr. Kelsoe was brought to this house. I do not believe it was truly for my husband's health, for he seemed to pay but little attention to that, yet I think it was for some scientific matter, for Dr. Kelsoe was always studying tables—quantities and calendars and so forth."

"Calendars?"

This was from Sandys.

"Yes, is that strange? I am sure that they were calendars. I looked over his shoulder once or twice and saw dates and the phases of the moon marked on his paper. And there were lists of things lying around in his room . . ."

"A vial of mercury? Cakes of glass?"

"Why, yes, how strange—I do recall those—and saltpeter and coals . . . and saffron . . . some quite ordinary things and others I had never heard of before."

"Did you ask him about them?"

"Yes, Dr. Sandys, I did, but he begged me not to press him. He said it was nothing, it would come to naught and he would have no more to do with it."

"Were those his words?"

"Yes, I recall them now."

She stopped for a moment, and seemed to tilt her head, almost as if she listened to a dead voice.

"But that conversation . . ."

"Yes?"

"It was about other matters altogether."

"Please tell us, Lady Jesmond," said Sandys. "You stand accused of murder; only the truth can help you now."

Ah, Murdoch Sandys, what an idealist you are, under that hardened Scottish medico's exterior!

But I said nothing, and she went on.

"Very well. I must admit that he, Dr. John Kelsoe . . ."

I took a guess. Guess? Damned certainty. Coop up a healthy young man in a house with a bored and beautiful woman whose elderly husband does not share her bed, shut them off from society, and why, 'tis a racing certainty they'll be tossing about between the sheets from sheer boredom, if for no more delicate feelings. Though there are many folk nowadays too mealy-mouthed to admit it, and young blood runs colder than it did in my day.

"You and Dr. Kelsoe, madam . . ."

And Clara Jesmond had to dress it all up a little.

"John Kelsoe was in love with me."

She got up out of her chair, as though confused for the moment by embarrassment, and a drift of scent reached me as she moved, an odor sweet and flowerlike, yet a stale, weary perfume. The room seemed airless; the talk of love something that came from another life.

"Please go on, Lady Jesmond."

She pulled back the closed curtains, and looked out of the window for a moment; put her hand to the latch of the casement, but did not open it. She then turned back into the room, and I saw that there were tears standing in her eyes, yet she did not break into weeping.

"John told me a few days after he came here that he had fallen passionately in love with me at first sight. For a while at least he desired nothing more than to be under the same roof as myself, and decided that he would say nothing and love me silently. But he could not carry out this resolution, and once, when we were in the drawing room alone, he fell upon my skirts and declared that he could not go a day further without speaking to me of his passion. And we became lovers, for a few days . . . and nights. He was utterly in love with me, you see. It was so . . . winning!"

Yes, it is the ultimate flattery, to be completely adored, to bask in absolute power, to have one's every whim a lover's command. Irresistible, to a bored, neglected creature, man or woman. Irresistible to Clara Jesmond.

"And was that how it was at the time of his death?"

"No."

She stood upright in front of the window and suddenly seemed less dreamy, as though there were another, stronger woman within her skin. Odds bobs! There was more to Clara Jesmond than I had thought.

"I had broken off with him."

She crossed the room again. The window remained unopened and the only air in the chamber seemed to be in the movement of her crumpled silks.

She flung herself down in the armchair and drew back into its depths.

"What had happened? Had your husband discovered the truth?"

"No, not then, though he did later. No, it was something else. Well, I suppose I must tell you."

She raised her head and looked at me almost with defiance.

"John Kelsoe wanted me to run away with him, to leave this house and go north somewhere, and live as man and wife. 'To spend my life with you!'—that's what he said. Precious little life he had left, as it turned out!"

She turned her head with its great tangle of fair hair toward the window, and murmured her next words.

"But I refused."

There was a pause.

"Your feelings for your husband—they were the cause?"

"I have to answer that question honestly. Otherwise we shall never understand this business at all, for our sentiments are at the heart of the matter, are they not?"

Yes, she was a more complicated woman than I had thought, as became increasingly apparent while I listened to her.

"Very well, the truth. It was *not* because of my feelings toward my husband, for they scarcely exist—they did once, but they are long dead. And nor was it fear of immorality, for that had not prevented me from becoming John's mistress. No . . ."

There was another pause. Not a word was uttered. The old house seemed to creak and shift.

There are moments when time stands still. As when a terrible truth is uttered.

"You must know, Lord Ambrose, that I would not run off with a penniless man!"

There—the truth was out.

So cold and harsh it sounded! She immediately began to justify it.

I had almost forgotten Mrs. Romey, but she had come out of a small side-room, probably my lady's dressing-room, during this exchange, and she came forward now as if to defend her charge. But Clara Jesmond continued with her own self-defense.

"Just consider, Lord Ambrose, here in this house I am Lady Jesmond. I have a position in society, I have everything I wish for—and with John Kelsoe I would have had nothing! He would have to find employment, and then we would have had to live off whatever meager earnings he could get . . . I am not used to such shifts, Lord Ambrose. I am not such a young woman anymore."

"So you refused to leave with him?"

"Yes. And I talked it over with my . . . with Mrs. Romey. She counseled me not to go. She said—"

The housekeeper seemed about to intervene, but Lady Jesmond gestured to her to remain silent and continued with her account of the unhappy passions of John Kelsoe, M.D., deceased.

"She said we had only to wait till Sir Antony died. That it could not be long—that his health was not good. Then I would inherit everything and I could marry whom I pleased, and I need sacrifice nothing."

"But your husband's will . . ."

"Yes, yes. Antony suspected something, and I think that is why he made that will, for it meant giving up everything if I should remarry. Or even if I should—" She paused.

"If you should take a lover."

This was Sandys, plain-speaking.

"So you rejected John Kelsoe?"

"Yes. He pleaded and pleaded with me, but I got angry with him. I told him I did not want a poverty-stricken creature such as he! Oh, I am so ashamed now of my words, but you see, I have known poverty in my life, Lord Ambrose, and I do not want it again, I assure you! It may be easy for those who have never known it to preach at me."

"I have absolutely no intention of preaching, Lady Jesmond. But then, what happened afterward? Did he accept what you said?"

"He appeared to. But it was the next day that he died."

"So he had a motive for suicide? The woman he adored had rejected him."

"I know it was suicide. He left me a note."

She got up, went to a portable writing desk that sat upon

a cabinet, turned the key in its gold lock, opened a drawer and extracted a sheet of paper. "This was the place where we exchanged messages. I found this paper here, after he died. He must have placed it here before he took that dreadful poison."

It was a short message, and a strange one: *love you to death and beyond: I cannot persuade you to be mine, but I can give you all you desire. That you shall have, I promise.*

There was a scrawled *J.* at the end.

CHAPTER 19

THE attitude of Sir Antony was the biggest obstacle in clearing Lady Jesmond from the charges against her, for when I intimated to him that the truth might be the only resource left, he was mightily offended and disappeared up the staircase to his room like some stringy old animal retreating to a den, its teeth still snarling at the world. Of Charnock, there was no sign.

Now matters were at such a pass that I determined to roust out all the secrets that this strange household tried so hard to keep hidden. Getting up in the middle of the night, my first purpose was to explore the attic at the top of the house—not the room where poor Kelsoe had died, but the other, with the new padlock upon the door.

"Sandys!" said I, rousing him from slumber.

He cursed with some Scottish oath, recondite and alarming, but followed me.

We slipped up the staircase.

As we neared the top of the stairs, I fancied I heard the

old boards creaking ahead of us. Upon the landing the moonlight outlined the door of Kelsoe's old room, standing wide open, no doubt as it had been left for the passage of his coffin through the doorway.

I held Sandys back.

Silence.

Then, again, a slight shifting sound.

Something else.

Some hand sliding a foul and secret poison into a hiding-place?

It was from close by.

Not from within the room itself.

I suddenly leaped forward and pulled the door toward me. Someone stumbled behind it, falling against the wall as if trying to vanish through it.

I seized the throat of the figure. Fat, fleshy. Not a ghost, most certainly; this living creature was distinctly and unpleasantly alive beneath my hand.

The intruder and I spun toward the window, where I allowed him to fall upon the floor, his face upturned in the moonlight shining full into Kelsoe's attic quarters.

It was the landlord of the Green Lion.

"Good God, man, what are you doing here?"

"No, Lord Ambrose, I beg you—don't call anyone!"

The man's face was twisted with fright. I dragged him upright, and Sandys shut the door behind us. The landlord was stammering with fright, but he managed to get out a coherent sentence at last.

"I saw it, you see. When he stopped for a drink."

"Who, man? Who stopped?"

"The carter, the one who came to Jesmond Place. It wasn't true, what I told you—that he said he couldn't delay."

I suddenly understood. "The man who was bringing a load of goods to this house? You said he drove straight on here."

"Yes. Well, it wasn't quite true."

This usually means "In fact, it was an out-and-out lie," and so it proved in this case, for the landlord went on: "He did stop at the Lion for a mug of ale. Said he'd come from Bristol without a break and his throat were as dry as a bone."

"But your wife said he wouldn't pause for a drink."

"That's what I told her, my lord. Naomi was upstairs when he came. So while he was having a sup in the bar . . ."

"What did you do?"

I had guessed, but I let him tell me. Confession is always more interesting than accusation; it is so much more informative.

"I went outside into the yard—he'd asked me to give the horse some feed—and I lifted up the cover on the cart. It was lashed down, but in one place it had come loose a bit—because of the jolting on the road, I suppose. Anyway, I pulled up a corner of it."

He added, pleadingly, "Just a few inches!"

"And what did you see, man?"

He stopped. Terrified yet somehow in the grip of a fascination, he stared at me, tension working in the muscles of his face, so that the fat cheeks were twitching involuntarily.

Yet it was not fear alone that possessed him. I could have sworn to that, for there was a look in his eyes as though he were gazing at something distant, yet extraordinary. It was the recollection of what he had seen. He was like a man remembering a vision.

Plainly, in the rough inn-yard, he had seen something that had changed his life.

He whispered the word.

"Gold. Pure gold, my lord. Lumps of it."

He moistened his lips. "Heaps of gold. As if it were just dug up out of the ground. Rocks of gold, with blisters and bubbles of gold in them. Just lying under the tarpaulin covering the cart. There in my yard."

"Oh, you idiot!" scoffed Sandys. "How can you have been so deluded! What made you think it could be gold?"

The landlord whispered again, as if overheard by some presence, as if the object of his desires had been a living thing invoked by his words. "It was in gleaming pieces, as if it had been quarried with a pick, not minted—all edges and pieces, yellow—like little mountains of gold. And—"

"And?"

I took a somewhat threatening step toward him, but it was not really necessary. He was possessed still by his vision, recounting it as if it had been a dream.

"I heard the fellow coming out toward the yard so I quickly covered up the cart again. The man came outside and climbed up on the cart and drove on—to this house, to Jesmond Place. So I—"

"You have come after it."

I finished the sentence for him.

The magic left his face. He became again a fat, terrified fool.

"I thought if I had just a little piece of it, just a tiny little piece of it, it would be enough to keep us for the rest of our lives. I didn't dare take any then—I thought the carter might check the load before he drove on."

"So you came here in search of it? As a thief, in fact."

"Oh, I beg your lordship, just let me go. Let me get back—I've never done anything like this before. Never even been tempted to. But there was something about it—the way it was heaped up there in that cart. As if it was thrown there for the taking. It's been in my mind ever since. I've never slept one night through without dreaming about it. And I got to thinking—it must be here somewhere, in Jesmond Place."

I looked at Sandys. The penalty for such an attempted theft was hanging. This silly innocent fellow, tempted to his death by what he had glimpsed beneath the cover of a cart in an inn-yard!

I stood aside and motioned toward the door.

The fellow started to escape.

Suddenly, I shot out a hand and grasped him by the collar.

"A word with you first," I hissed in his ear.

I don't know what he was expecting, but my question clearly surprised him.

"The name of your inn, the Green Lion. Where does that name come from? I have never heard of any inn or alehouse in the length or breadth of the country with such a name. Did you call it that?"

He was taken aback.

"The name, my lord? Why, there's nothing in the name! I do believe it's been called that for more'n two hundred year—since old Charnock came to Combwich. They say he stayed in the inn at first, before he had a house in the village."

"Charnock?"

"Yes, my lord. This young fellow who's here now—his family's from Combwich. Old Thomas Charnock must have been his great-grandfather, or great-great—I can't count 'em. They hands things down, in that family. Didn't you know? The young fellow's from these parts."

It had never occurred to me to wonder where Charnock had sprung from. Nor to Sandys either, or so I judged by the expression on his face.

But what the landlord said next, as he squirmed to get away from me, was even more astonishing.

"Ask Dr. Henderson, my lord. He lives in Charnock's house."

Henderson!

Open-mouthed, I let go of the landlord's sweaty collar and he slipped like a fat wraith through the doorway.

But I knew now what lay at the heart of this corruption. "It's here, somewhere," I whispered, "and if we find it, we'll save an innocent woman from the gallows."

"And a fool from his folly," added my companion.

"Oh Sandys, we are on no moral crusade! If men derive pleasure from being gulled, let them proceed! But we need some proof of what is going on, and I believe I know something of this Dr. Henderson. Let me go and speak with him, and perhaps I can coax a few things out of him."

Sandys spoke hastily as we hurried downstairs.

"Lord Ambrose, do not be impetuous," he hissed. "Remember you are not now on some wild Greek island. This is the English countryside!"

"Yes, I will take care to bear in mind that I am not among civilized people and to behave with corresponding savagery."

"I am always most fearful when your lordship is most flippant, for I fear the grain of truth in your humor."

"Thank you, Sandys." By this time, we had reached a back door; dawn was breaking outside and a blackbird whistled its sharp call of alarm as I opened it. A chorus of hedge-birds, ragged but exceeding loud, near-deafened us, but seemed to leave Jesmond Place and its occupants unawakened and unmoved.

"There is still some time before the household will be stirring, Sandys. Will you keep watch over Lady Jesmond to ensure her safety, while I ride to Combwich to find this Henderson?"

I did not, this time, dignify Henderson with the title of "Dr."

Thus I left Sandys, with a rug wrapped around him, sitting in the passageway outside her ladyship's chamber in the early dawn light, wondering why he was being such a fool as to get himself into this situation . . . and shuffling about to get into a more comfortable position.

CHAPTER 20

THE village of Combwich was as I remembered it, anonymous, slumbering in the early light. If the church at Otterhampton had been a mouse asleep, this village resembled a lazy gray cat stretched out from nose to tail, down to the tidal creek on the river.

The head, so as to speak, was the Green Lion, which stood at one end of the long curving street. This, the village thoroughfare, which I had glimpsed on my first journey to Jesmond Place, culminated in a narrowed bottleneck winding up the hillside, which was the tail of the sleeping cat, to continue my fanciful analogy. The houses overlooked the river, where there was an old timbered dock stretching out into the water, or pressed up opposite each other so that the villagers must look into one another's windows, were there any activities of interest to observe, which had seemed a remote possibility, I must confess. The town might once have been quite a little port: it snoozed quietly now, gently sleeping on mud and rock.

But I had misjudged Combwich. Something was evidently stirring here.

At the Green Lion, the sign with its painted pea-green beast creaked gently in a breeze; the landlord's wife was up and about early in the yard, pegging out sheets and wearing a fine pair of scarlet shoes as she danced back and forth across the dusty yard with her laundry. She greeted me with no trace of embarrassment or hint of what might have passed with her husband after we had released him and he had bolted like a rabbit from Jesmond Place. Probably, she had been innocent of his attempt to gain a portion of the "gold" for himself. She had not seen that glittering substance with her own eyes; perhaps she remained untainted.

I did not think of it as real gold; I knew what it was. Suddenly, that one word, the name of Henderson, had clicked into place as smoothly as a key turning the tumblers of a great lock, and I understood what was happening at Jesmond Place.

She directed me to Charnock's house.

"A little way outside the village, alongside the river, my lord. An old place, all on its own there. You won't mistake it."

Yes, all on its own. That fitted the puzzle, too. Like Friar Bacon's tower in Oxford, just on the edge of the town.

One of them had lived there, long after Bacon.

They were recommended to have isolated dwellings, in those old books.

The houses overlooked the way, and the air hung dusty and stale between them. Here and there, a face was distinguishable within, swimming like a pale fish in the darkness of some tiny room, moving to stare as I passed, some of the dwellings so low I could not see into the lower rooms at all. Zaraband danced down, graceful even on the steep, unsure footing, like a creature in a dream, as indeed she must have appeared to the watching eyes within those houses.

We reached the last narrow houses of the huddle and swung left to follow the bank. Beyond, a small stream ran across our path, with a ramshackle bridge over it, and just beyond the bridge was a tall gray-stone house, bigger than any of the village dwellings, and clearly set apart from them.

"You won't mistake it." That was what the landlady had said.

As I drew nearer, I could see the door was painted, worn and peeling, but still visible as a dull orange-red, and upon it were markings in black. Moons, circles topped with crosses, three radiant suns grouped in a triangle.

I rapped upon the door.

The man who answered my knock was taller than I am, with old bones as worn and fine as carving beneath his paper-white face. He could not hold himself upright under the lintel of the painted door.

A tattered fur cloak hung about his hunched shoulders.

I was struck with a kind of sorrow to see this: the betrayal of a fine mind; the shipwrecked old age of a fiery intelligence. I had a reluctance to apprehend the fullness of the disaster which had overtaken him.

He looked up into my face, for what seemed a very long time, and the black pupils of his eyes seemed to sink deep into my mind, but I knew it was a trick to hold my gaze, a habit put on with his conjuror's cloak. So I stared back, and he flinched and spoke first, and it was a small kind of victory. But I was startled by his words.

"I knew you would come."

"Do you know me, then?"

"No. But I know you are the man who will end it. I see it

in your face. To tell you the truth, it is a relief to me, at last, to have done."

We entered the dark hallway.

"My study is upstairs. I get more light for the work, when I need it. I keep it dark, mostly."

At the top of the stone steps was a square chamber, and there he took me. Almost led me, for my eyes were still unaccustomed to the dim light. Gradually, the dazzling ceased.

I was in a room hung with black and gold, shutting out the light, with a curtain stretching over the outline of a window. Henderson cannot have needed much light recently. A small breeze fluttered the edge of the blackness.

He stood and paused, as if he expected to deliver a speech, but I gave him no opportunity. I knew now what "the work" was.

"Yes, I have come to end it."

There was no point in delaying.

I strode across and tore down the curtain. It was rotten: it came away at one pull and fell with a heap of cracked plaster, old curtain rings and spiders, all upon the floor. The dawn light poured in.

I heard the old man cry out behind me.

The black velvet of the walls was revealed in the daylight as shabby, dusty, faded to brown streaks in places. And now I could see that a table covered with a deep crimson cloth stood in one corner of the room.

"Very well, damn you! See it all!"

With a dramatic gesture, Henderson crossed to the table and pulled the cloth off.

Beneath it lay a great glass flask, and within that, floating on some thick green liquid, were the heads of two children. One seemed to have a ruddy dark red-gold countenance and flaxen hair: the other a face of albino white and long silver locks that floated on the viscous surface.

Even I turned aside in horror. The atrocities of war, these I have seen, men tortured, cut apart, dreadful deeds done in the heat. But such deliberate, careful dismemberment of the innocent . . . I forced myself to look again.

They were of wax. Carefully modeled and painted, the lips tinted in red, a mass of wig-hair attached to the unnaturally glistening scalps.

The old man sat down and bowed his head.

"Who are you? I do not know your name."

"Ambrose Malfine."

I sat down opposite him. He was at an end, but I could take my time. We both knew it.

He started at my name. "I have heard of you. They said at Oxford that you were the most brilliant student of your generation—and that you fled the place. Well, I cannot blame you."

"And you are Dr. Henderson, once the most gifted of scholars in the University, the leading light of science. And now . . ."

I gazed round and gestured at the tawdry furnishings; the shelf of dirty glass, vials, retorts, alembics, presented an ironic mockery of the orderly rows of vessels I had seen ranged in Daubeny's laboratory in Oxford. Above the shelf, the neat rows of scientific books I had seen there were parodied in Henderson's "laboratory" by an untidy row of grubby, dog-eared folios. This was the black knowledge, the mock science, that destroyed its own practitioners with its greed and folly.

"And now, you are an alchemist. That is to say a fraudster,

a trickster, a man with whom a fairground conjuror compares most favorably! How much does Sir Antony pay you?"

The yellowish lips parted in a sort of laugh.

"More than science does, my dear young fellow!"

"You caught him with your false promises. I suppose you told him you could—what is it you and your fellows claim to do? To change base metals into gold?"

"Yes, Ambrose, but it would be true to say also that he trapped me with his money. I was a poor man, remember, born to a humble family, and given a miserable pittance at Oxford. Oh, I started out quite innocently. I was making an exploration of arcane science, of medieval studies such as the writings of Friar Bacon."

That was what had alerted me. Friar Bacon's tower, at Oxford. And who had lived there later but another student of the esoteric and occult sciences! The name lingered so irritatingly at the back of my mind.

"And you studied the works of his successors, I presume. Such as the man who lived in Bacon's tower in Oxford, who was supposed to be a magus—or some say, a magician. An alchemist, was he not?"

"Yes, the very same. He was known as the last English alchemist, but that is not true, of course. There were later ones. Charnock lived in Bacon's tower, but he left Oxford and came back to the West Country where he was born. And he came here, to Combwich. This was Charnock's own house."

I was startled.

"But that was two and a half centuries ago, was it not? Then who is the fellow at Jesmond Place, the pale-faced little creature who trails around the house?"

"Another Charnock, his descendant. I came here, you see,

in pursuit of the older Charnock's work. I thought something written might survive—I was curious as to what experiments on metals he might have conducted, and so forth."

"Was that why you left Oxford?" I asked.

"Yes, I left Oxford for Bristol. Bristol, you know, was where the alchemist Samuel Norton came from. He was much more famous than old Charnock, and I originally went to see if I could find out anything about him. But there seemed no remaining trace of Norton—and then I learned that Charnock had been in these parts also. And so I came here and found this house, just as he had left it, with all his books and his vessels. They had shut everything up. He had married a local woman, and his family still lived in the house. Everyone had been afraid to touch his things—they were just country people round here, full of superstitions. There were still his drawings on the walls, and astronomical figures marked upon the doors. These wax heads were old Charnock's—and these velvet hangings here. His descendant, the young man who is now at Jesmond Place, was sitting in this very room when I first came here. He was trying to understand the books, you see."

He pointed to the row of dusty blackish leather-bound volumes.

I walked round the room and pulled a book off the shelves at random.

The Key of Alchemy by Samuel Norton, 1577.

I flipped through the stained and dusty old pages. Some things I could make partial sense of. The male and female principles which create the Philosopher's Stone—those, I take it, were represented in Henderson's lair by the nasty waxwork heads, which might persuade the credulous if displayed in a dim light. There was something else I recognized: some of the woodcuts had been colored over and there were various creatures, a deer, a snake, and a fierce-looking beast carefully painted in a vitriolic shade: "the Green Lion." The village inn had been connected with old Charnock.

Henderson saw me looking at the illustration.

"The Green Lion is a symbol for mercury. Old Charnock persuaded the landlord of the inn to change his sign; it was the Golden Lion originally—quite a usual name. People would come here looking for Charnock, you see, wanting to consult the alchemist, and the Green Lion was a secret sign for them, that they had come to the right village. Then they would be directed to this house. But the present landlord is an innocent fool—he knows nothing of alchemy!"

He knew nothing of it, yet it had corrupted him, I thought. The power of riches, that one glimpse of fool's gold when he lifted the cover on the cart, had made a thief out of an honest man. And possibly a murderer, too, for was this business in any way connected with the deaths of Kelsoe and young Cyriack Jesmond?

I looked again at the book. The words were jumbles, muddled Latin and Greek. "The Kerotakis," I read. "The Litharge."

"Good God man! What rubbish is this? Surely you cannot have been deceived by it!"

"You are in the right, Malfine, it is mere conjuration. Yet Charnock's descendant was trying to puzzle it out. He could not decipher it—he could not read the Greek, for a start. There he was, having inherited all this wealth of learning, as he thought, and he could make nothing of it, country boy that he was."

"So the older Charnock had not passed his knowledge on?"

"No. Thomas Charnock had been one of the most scholarly men of his generation, corrupt though that learning was. But it seems he chose not to teach his son, who was skeptical in all these matters, and though he intended to give instruction to his grandson, he died suddenly when the boy was still a child. So there was his family, buried in the depths of the countryside with this alchemist's laboratory and these books, yet they could make nothing of it. Young Charnock could barely read and write when I came here."

"And you taught him?"

"Yes, he was an apt pupil—and then it was he who conceived the idea that we might—"

"That you might try to revive the science of alchemy and gull some wealthy local fool into parting with his money."

"Yes, that was the idea—just to ask him for a little money, at first, anyway. But Charnock did not want to go to Jesmond Place at first. He thought it was safer to stay here, because—"

"Because, if he were found out to be defrauding Sir Antony Jesmond, then it would be best to remain at a safe distance?"

"Exactly. But things did not turn out the way we planned."

"I imagine not. Tell me about Kelsoe—he did not turn out as you planned, did he? Did he discover what you were up to?"

"No, he was supposed to be the one who actually conducted the experiments for Sir Antony. He was engaged to do so; Charnock and I were going to remain here and act as advisers in his work."

"But Kelsoe refused?"

"Yes, when he knew what it was. He was asked to come as personal physician to Sir Antony, and then to work on the experiment . . . but he said he would not prostitute himself so! He said he had taken the Hippocratic oath of the physician not to misuse his knowledge and that alchemy was fraudulent, a false science. But in any case . . ."

"In any case, the unfortunate young fellow is as dead as a doornail!"

"Oh, I perceive your meaning—but we did nothing to harm poor Kelsoe. Why, I greatly regret his death. That I swear to you, Ambrose. Yes, Charnock and I took money from Sir Antony, promising him we could turn lead and iron into gold, but murder? Never! When Kelsoe died, Charnock took over and stepped into his shoes, tending the experiment for Sir Antony. It cannot be left to go out, you see, the alchemical furnace. That is what the books say: the process takes sixty days, and it must be tended constantly during that period."

"But you do not believe this nonsense, Henderson! You were a man of reason, of science! How can you believe that this mumbo-jumbo will produce gold in sixty days? You must know that many have claimed to do so, yet no one has ever achieved it, and we know indubitably from the science of chemistry that it is impossible. Come, man, use your intelligence!"

The old man sagged in his chair. I saw a conflict in his face and understood that he might be the victim of his own deceptions: that he had perhaps come to believe the nonsense he had been promulgating.

"Malfine, I no longer know what I believe. But that was what I told Sir Antony—what I learned from the books. That to make gold the furnace must burn for twice thirty days. It was why Sir Antony wanted to have it at Jesmond Place, instead of here in my house, so that he could watch and wait. He wanted to be there at the exact moment it happened; that was what seemed to grasp his imagination. The moment when he would look into the vessel and see it. See the gold we had created."

Henderson's old eyes were fixed and staring: he seemed almost himself to see that magical moment after sixty days and nights of laboring over the stinking compounds of yellow sulfur and black and red salts, the bowl of mercury, the tiny fiery furnace, the smoky glass vessels, when the alchemist would lead his credulous victim to the crucible, and there, before the wondering gaze would be a glorious treasure, a heap of pure, gleaming gold, where before there had been a gray dirty mass.

Such was the "chymical art" described in these old books of demi-sorcery.

Such was the conjuring trick that Henderson and Charnock had prepared to play upon Sir Antony Jesmond.

I, Ambrose Malfine, thought that I had become hardened to this world, yet I gazed at Henderson with a mixture of pity and anger. What a brave and clever mind this had been! "What a noble mind is here o'erthrown!" A revolutionary, cleaving a brave new path in science as in politics, and yet he had deserted everything, broken his faith, betrayed his belief in reason. Not, surely, because he himself was fool enough to believe in this preposterous alchemical prancing, but because he had led others into folly.

Not just Sir Antony Jesmond, whom he had gulled for money. Henderson had done far worse: I thought of the young child, Charnock, growing up in this remote country village, thirsting to read, hungry for knowledge, looking for someone, anyone, who could teach him. And what had Henderson, the scholar, given that child? Had he taught him languages, sciences, passed on to him some true and rational knowledge? No, he had fed him on pap, rubbish, worthless incantations—a mish-mash of half-learning. I loathed the man, I confess, though I did not hate Charnock, the unfortunate child who had grown up under Henderson's tutelage.

He sat there, his white hair flowing over the absurd and moth-eaten old fur cloak, and put his head in his hands. "Malfine, what will you do?"

I laughed out loud. "Do? Treat you as you deserve. You may be implicated in murder—how can one believe your protestations? Why should anyone take the word of a known fraud and deceiver? Why should anyone believe that you did not kill poor Kelsoe when he found out what you were involved in and refused to be a party to it? And having killed once, why not again? Perhaps Cyriack Jesmond discovered something of his father's alchemical folly—and perhaps he resented his inheritance being thrown away upon such tricksters."

"No, no, I heard about young Jesmond's death, but it had nothing to do with us—with what we were engaged in! And neither did the death of Dr. Kelsoe, although he had nothing but contempt for us, that is true! We took money from Sir Antony; we took gold, telling him that some gold was needed for the experiment, as a crop needs to grow from seed. But murder, no! Do not think that of me, I beg you, Malfine."

His face looked up, spittle clinging to his old lips, fear in his eyes. A fraud, a liar, a cheat. But a murderer? I looked round the study: there among the tubes and flasks, the evil-smelling paraphernalia of deceit, might lurk many strange poisons, poisons that could kill a man yet leave him lying as tranquil as if he had just fallen asleep. Henderson could not be allowed the chance of escape, perhaps to commit more murder, if his brilliant mind had descended into such an abyss.

But I had little time, I reflected, to act as village constable here. I needed to get back to Jesmond Place, not only to warn Sir Antony of the deceptions practiced upon him, but to ensure the safety of Clara Jesmond, in that house of greed and lunacy.

I looked out of the window. It was small, high up. Then I looked across to the door and saw an old iron key in the lock.

"The wrath of those who have been fooled by alchemists is terrible, when once they find they have been deceived. The world is full of cheated gulls and pig-widgeons, but beware of them when they discover the truth! It is not much more than a century since Caetano was executed in Germany for promising some petty princeling he could make gold from lead. Do you know what they did there? When they found out he was a fraud, they hanged him on a gilded gallows! If Sir Antony finds out the truth, then I advise you to stay safely within your house, without venturing out. And to make sure you follow my advice, I'll lock you in. Now I'll leave you here, Henderson, and counsel you not to try to escape. How can you hope to hide in a country district such as this, where everyone will know you, and every mouth will mock you? Better stay here—locked safely in!"

Henderson shuddered; he said no more, pleaded no further, but bowed his head. I slammed the door of the alchemist's lair, and the key grated in the iron lock, but there might well be another way out of the house.

It was my intention to send for a constable to keep guard

over him, just in case there was another means of escape or the lock was as old and rusty as the rest of this decaying house, or at least to summon a stout villager armed with a cudgel or some other crude rustic skull-cracker, but at that moment someone came puffing along the village street, a personage I had last seen in the attics of Jesmond Place, or to be exact, bouncing arsy-varsy down the stairs away from the said attics.

It was the landlord of the Green Lion, slipping along as quietly as his bulk would allow, evidently suffering a conflict between his curiosity and his fear. I put him out of his misery.

"If you want to redeem yourself—you see that house at the end?"

He answered reluctantly, but from the way he looked sideways along the street, he evidently knew what I meant. "Dr. Henderson's house, my lord?"

"Exactly. Now you are to stand outside it, and if Henderson tries to come out, you are to . . . to make him go back in." I eyed the unarmed and quivering prospective agent of the law and, observing a long implement leaning against a garden wall, I seized it. "Here, take this . . . whatever it is."

"Dibbler, my lord."

"Quite. Now wave this at him if there's any trouble."

His face was white, though. The dibbler would not solve all his troubles. He muttered the next words, surely the strangest ever heard in an English village street.

"My lord, what if he . . . what if he . . . *flies?*"

Good God, what stories had been circulating in this quiet little English place? I suddenly got a glimpse into a world of village fears, of a tissue of stories and rumors that must have been resounding through the cottages and yards.

"Now listen to me. Henderson is just an old man. A man, d'you hear, like any other—like you or me. He cannot fly. He cannot change base metals into gold. He has no magic powers of any kind. Come with me."

I pulled him, sweating as he was, back down the street, into the house, up the stairs and into the alchemist's lair. The sun was shining into the room; the curtains lay where they had fallen. Henderson was still sitting in his chair, and in the sunshine now he looked exactly like any other rheumy-eyed old man, his mouth dribbling a little.

The landlord of the Green Lion cried out at the sight of the heads in the jar, but with one blow I smashed it to the floor and the waxy heads bounced about like nasty little dolls.

"See, it's all trickery! Playthings for a mad old man. You have nothing at all to fear."

And to Henderson: "This man will be outside the door if you try to escape."

He looked up vacantly, and nodded. I don't think he even really saw us then. My intention was to stiffen the resolve of his guardian.

It might not have worked. The "constable" was not of promising material. But he stared at the room, at the shabby hangings and the dusty books and the broken heap of wax and glass on the floor. Then he turned to me, and his plump body seemed to relax suddenly; the color came back to his face.

"So this is all it was? What them stories were all about? An old fellow and a pile of rubbish?"

"All it was," said I.

CHAPTER 21

JESMOND Place seemed older and more rotten than ever, crepuscular even on a summer's day. I repressed my instincts to leap from Zaraband's back, stride up the steps and break open the battered silvery timbers of the door.

In Greece, when I had two or three times led a rescue mission to prise one of my lieutenants from the torturing grip of an enemy prison, I had discovered caution, unnatural though it is to my impetuous temperament. Impetuous, yes, but not idiotic.

So as we entered the drive I nudged Zaraband on to the grass at the verge, and her hoofs clipped silently along on the soft earth. I took the precaution, even, of wrapping a kerchief round the rings of the bit: probably, there would be no need of that, but when I revert to my capacity as silent and efficient assassin, I carry out all the steps of my training. Nothing must be overlooked, for the difference between slitting a man's guts and having your own entrails kabobbed may be a matter of a hair's breadth. Or of the tiny warning jingle of a horse's bit heard through an open window.

And as I slid from Zaraband's back before the entrance, my knife somehow slipped automatically into my left palm, so accustomed was I to its use: there I held it, the blade pointing upward. That is the sign of a trained killer, by the way: hold your blade point up, aim it in the right place, clasp the foe in a tight embrace, and the victim will do half your work for you by conveniently impaling his heart upon the knife.

In Greece I learned skills which I cannot now unlearn.

Nor would I. They are needed in England too.

There was the trace of a thick, greasy-looking smoke coming from one of the chimneys, so there was something alive in the house, even if it were only a fire.

Moving silently down to the kitchens: empty, silent. All left in good order by Mrs. Romey. The kitchen grate quite cold and even cleared of ashes. Still-rooms, butler's pantry, doors yielding easily to a push from my boot. Nothing.

The great hall, scene of funeral feasts, empty. No fire had burned here for some months, I judged: there were even some recent twigs and feathers fallen into the fireplace from a nest somewhere up in the vast chimney above the fireplace.

My unease should have been soothed by these tokens of emptiness. Instead, it increased.

Up the stairs, taking three or four at a stride with my absurdly long legs, which minimized the creaking of the warped old stair-treads. Once, there was the sharp crack of protesting old wood, and I crouched on the step. No one appeared to challenge my intrusion. Someone should have done so. Sandys should have done so. I had left him on guard outside Clara Jesmond's room.

In Lady Jesmond's chamber her ladyship doubtless slumbered on; at least, there was no sound from the room. Nevertheless, I thought I should just confirm that all was well with her ladyship.

I rapped gently on her door, and called her name softly. There was no answer, and I knocked again and called that of Mrs. Romey, thinking that at this late hour in the morning she would be awake and in attendance on her mistress.

There was still no response. I turned away from the door and looked about me, and saw only the silent dark emptiness of Jesmond Place stretching away down the stairs into the black unlit pit of the hall. At that moment I felt that Jesmond Place had finished its time as a source of life and shelter, and that it now had to offer only hatred and death, which seemed to well up in the depths beneath me.

I turned the handle of Lady Jesmond's door very cautiously, and found that the door opened beneath my hand. It had surely been locked before. I inched my way into the room, fearing to disturb her ladyship if she still slumbered, yet with a sinking heart. My senses seemed to tell me the room was empty: I heard no quiet breathing, no gentle rustling sounds of life.

Nothing at all.

Was it possible that Lady Jesmond had fallen victim to murder? There was but a faint light coming from the landing, where I had left the door ajar, and a few rays of sunlight that slipped in through a narrow gap in the heavy curtains. I could just make out the massive bulk of the old furniture and some heaped and twisted linen upon the bed. Crossing to the window, I drew back the curtains; daylight streamed in.

Empty.

There was a door leading off one side of the room into the little alcove, her ladyship's dressing-room. I flung it open, wide.

Still nothing. Beside an empty china cup and saucer, a little silver kettle stood on a tiny spirit stove. I touched it: the sides were still warm. Mrs. Romey, it seemed, had been about to make her ladyship a hot drink. But both women, Lady Clara Jesmond and her housekeeper, had effectively vanished, along with their protector, Murdoch Sandys.

Perhaps they were still somewhere in some part of this rambling old rabbit-warren. I feared for them, yet neither Kelsoe nor Cyriack Jesmond had been abducted; both had been killed exactly where they were, Kelsoe in his own bed, Cyriack on his horse. The hand of a poisoner surely did not need to drag its victims out of their beds: it had more effective ways of dispatching them.

Where to start? The obvious place. If my lady had fled for some reason, where else should she go but to her husband for protection.

I crossed the landing and turned the door handle of Sir Antony's bedchamber as quietly as I could. The door swung open quite easily, and I was in Sir Antony's sanctum.

It was an old-fashioned room, even by my own unfashionable standards. The curtains were open, so presumably Sir Antony had risen, and sunshine warmed the old mahogany furniture, massive pieces in a dark wine color. A turkey carpet with a faded pattern lay on the floor, black-framed steel engravings of some classical temple hung over the mantel. Sir Antony seemed to have imposed no particular taste at all upon his room. There was no desk, no books, no papers: no signs of study here.

I moved on, round the other side of the vast bed. A small

room stood beyond, with a wash-stand, razor-strop and so forth, the mere necessities. Some old and anonymous-looking clothes were hanging in a wardrobe.

Nothing here. I slipped out of the room and paused on the stairs before ascending to the attic floors.

The door to Kelsoe's room, where the landlord of the Green Lion had been discovered hiding, stood wide-open still. I pushed it back cautiously against the wall: no one was concealed behind it this time, and no one awaited me in the dead man's room.

I glanced toward the other attic door; the padlock upon it was now hanging loose. The door pushed easily open, without a sound. The carpenter had oiled the hinges well, no doubt under careful instruction and the wood moved slowly but silently under my hand.

I had a view of the whole length of a long room, the most extraordinary I had ever seen, under the eaves of the house. It was fitted up almost like a laboratory, with a long bench on one side covered with vials and flasks. At the far end, under the chimney-breast, was built a small furnace of a strange design, almost like an oven, or the kiln I once saw in a glassblower's workplace in Bristol. I could see the live charcoal which supplied the heat, burning with a dark-red glow beneath a black metal grill, and from time to time came a hissing and spitting of the coals, which mingled with the sounds of bubbling merging from various beakers and tubes. There was an unpleasant smell in the air, a dry, chemical odor. I had to stifle a cough.

Halfway along one of the benches sat two people. Their backs were turned, but I recognized Sir Antony Jesmond and his assistant, Mr. Charnock; they were deeply absorbed in something.

On the other side of the room, on a common wooden bench, lay a substance whose reflections dazzled across floor and ceiling, a golden glistening lump of matter, a glittering miniature yellow mountain of magical tiny rocks and caves.

Sir Antony was saying to Charnock: "But surely it must be ready by now! Thirty days, that was what you promised!"

Pieces of glass from some broken tube or beaker lay on the floor at their feet. Plainly, there had been some argument.

Charnock was wringing his hands; I could see that his eyes were watery, with reddened rims, as if his face had been exposed to smoke or fiery heat. "Sir Antony, we cannot hasten the process! The gross work, the preparation of the Philosopher's Stone, is complete, yet there is most of the subtle work still to undergo. I must explain that to you: the gross work is to make the Stone, the litharge, from sulfur and quicksilver—with other secret minerals which I have supplied—and that first step we have achieved. And the subtle work, which will actually make the gold itself by means of the Stone, has already produced this wonder that we have here upon the bench. But we must have another thirty days!"

"I was hoping for more." Sir Antony's voice was thin and quavery, like his shanks, yet had a reedy and horrible determination in it, like the strength of a piano wire.

Charnock's reply came swift and smooth.

"We cannot expect results quite so soon. Old Jabir, the Arab alchemist, said that to produce major results must require a further thirty moons. But consider what we have already achieved!"

And here Charnock, who looked to my medical eye as though he had been a rheumaticky child, his chest narrow, his spine concave, swung round and gestured in the direction of the gleaming substance lying on the bench behind them and uttered his single word of incantatory magic.

"Gold!"

At which Sir Antony, too, turned around. He reached out and caressed the pale yellow shiny mass, which was about a foot high, and then stepped up close, his face staring down upon it. I have never seen a man touch unfeeling, bloodless matter in such a way: I could see quite plainly that he was in love with the stuff, wanted to adore it, to treat it like a woman for whom he had a terrible passion.

That the man should let himself become such a fool! I could stand it no longer. Stepping forth into the room, I cried out: "Do you think that is gold, Sir Antony? How on earth have you been deceived into such idiocy? Why, the simplest schoolboy could not be taken in!"

Charnock gave a shout of alarm, and backed away from me toward the furnace at the far end of the room. Sir Antony spun round, away from the gleaming mass.

"Lord Ambrose! What are you doing here—and how dare you creep around my house in this fashion!"

"I dare, Sir Antony, because someone has to tell you the truth, and you should be grateful! Oh, I can see what this fellow has been doing. Alchemy—is that not it? He has convinced you he can turn base metal into gold, you poor fool."

"He has done it, I tell you! Look here! This is the gold he made from a mass of lead!"

"Gold? You would find more valuable stuff in a midden!"

Sir Antony's face was contorted now with a terrible rage, the anger of a man who knows he is about to be cheated of his dream. He almost screamed at me: "Get out, get out of here! What do *you* know of these matters? You're just a damned ignoramus who can't believe the evidence of your own eyes!"

I walked across to the bench.

"Evidence, Sir Antony? You call this evidence?"

He caught me by the arm, speaking passionately now.

"Yes, can't you see what it is, Malfine? Gold—pure gold! And he can make more. He is making more even now—there it is, hanging above the furnace!"

And he waved with a hand that held something sharp and gleaming, toward a blackened substance suspended within an iron contrivance over the charcoal which burned at the far end of the room. As I advanced the length of the room, I saw that beside it lay something which filled me with utter horror. Trussed and lashed down, gagged so that the faintest of its frantic sounds were quite lost beside the crackling and hissing of the furnace, was a human form. Next to it the blackened mass was glowing red in places, streaked with an acid green in others.

"That is lead which will turn to gold! It must be treated thus, bathed in Roman vitriol, and heated for thirty days and nights. At any moment now, it will change, and we shall find a golden mass! And as for your companion here—we shall dispose of him!"

It was Sandys, his eyes turning desperately toward me.

"It must have blood!" Sir Antony was mumbling. "The work must have blood to seal the gold—Charnock says so. A cockerel or a cat would have done, but human blood is better, you see, Malfine. Charnock, just give me the word; all is ready if the moment is right."

Not the least horrible thing about this statement was

that it was delivered in a flat, soft voice, with no trace of feeling left in it. Sir Antony, I perceived, was now truly insane, turned into something not human by the hunt for gold.

My instinct of course was to leap forward and cut my friend free, but I could not afford to indulge that impulse, because the bright object which Sir Antony held was a cutthroat razor, ready to slice through the artery with the slightest pressure of the crazy hand that held it. Of course, I could overcome both the aged Sir Antony and the feeble form of Charnock, but Sir Antony would reach his intended victim sooner. I cursed myself that I had not brought my pistol. Damnable pride, thought I. Ambrose Malfine, you believed you needed no aid! Well, see now, your friend will pay for it!

Perhaps I could talk some sense into Jesmond. "Oh, you poor idiot!" I called aloud. "Charnock and Henderson have really made a fool of you. Gold? This is mere iron, my dear sir, a form of iron which is almost as worthless as stone! It looks like gold, it gleams and glitters—and it is worth nothing. Nothing at all. That is what you have on this bench, believe me. Have you never heard of pyrite? Why, it can be dug up like potatoes, even in Devonshire! Fool's gold, Jesmond—fool's gold!"

I was advancing as I spoke, trying to observe their reactions. Charnock, I perceived, was not so far down the path of insane greed as Sir Antony. I could see by his face that he realized the murderous situation in which his alchemical web of deceit had trapped him.

"Charnock!" I urged. "For God's sake, tell him to throw away that razor! Jesmond will obey you—he will do anything you tell him is needed to get gold. Explain that blood is *not* needed—or that you can get it some other way. Think, man! If he kills Sandys, it will be at your urging, and you will both be guilty of murder. Call him off!"

Charnock stood irresolute for a few moments, his pale face turned toward the scene at the end of the attic, where poor Sandys could but plead for his life with his eyes alone. The razor glinted in the reddish light of the furnace. Sir Antony's feverish eyes were fixed on Charnock's face, waiting for a signal.

I had never really thought of Charnock as a full human being; he had been just a shadow trailing through the house behind his master, Antony Jesmond. Did he have a conscience, a heart? What had his early training at the hands of that strange creature, Henderson, done to him, this country fellow with his strange heritage of corrupted learning? I saw a young face there, sunken and white, yet the face of a boy still, rather than a grown man. "You should not overlook anyone, Malfine," I chided myself. "You thought he was an insignificant wretch, a weakling, yet here he has the power of life or death. And you have learned nothing about him, except the barest bones of his life! Perhaps he is as mad as his master."

That pause haunts me yet. It was a mere second or two, yet it seemed to stretch out for eternity, so that ahead lay death, grief, and the horrible physical reality of the bright spurting arterial blood, the slackening body, the life of a friend vanishing before my eyes. All these I had seen before, in my other life, and thought to see them now again, yes, and the widow's tears also.

Charnock spoke, very quietly and carefully.

"No, Sir Antony. We do not need blood now. You will have your gold without it. Put down the razor. Put it down on the bench."

Sir Antony looked down at the razor in his hand, as if trying to understand a secret sign that lay upon it.

The hand holding the razor did not move. It gripped it still. Then Sir Antony raised it and said, "No, Charnock. You are afraid. What a coward you are!"

And he moved toward Sandys, whose eyes were pleading in desperation.

For a moment, I did not comprehend what happened next, though my eyes took in the extraordinary sight of Sir Antony spinning back against the wall, of the razor flying through the air and landing harmlessly on the floor, of delicate glass objects shattering and leaping from the benches. And my ears suffered the sound of a deafening explosion which hurtled all around the walls of that confined space.

Someone had fired a shot from the far end of the room.

I spun round.

Charnock was gaping at something behind me.

She was still gripping the weapon, though her arm had dropped to her side. The frothing lace of her sleeve was blackened with powder.

She came across the room, her buckled riding-boots crunching on the broken glass, and held out the pistol.

"Your weapon, I believe. You left it behind at Malfine, Ambrose. Please remember it in future. I cannot always guarantee to get you out of a scrape."

Elisabeth Anstruther laughed and her yellow eyes were looking up into mine, with an exhilarated defiance.

When I turned again to the scene behind us, I saw that blood had welled up on Sir Antony's jacket, but he was not mortally wounded. We did not attempt to stop him from leaving, nor did Charnock hinder me as with my own knife I cut Sandys free. But as my friend struggled clear, the crucible on the furnace overturned, and the substance therein shot up in a mighty sheet of flame as it fell on the charcoal, barring our way to the attic door beyond.

Sandys was the quickest thinker, in spite of his ordeal.

"There's another way out, Miss Anstruther, Malfine! That's how I got up here!"

And he dragged us through the smoke to a narrow door at the other end of the attic; within moments we were stumbling down a narrow twisting staircase cut within the old walls of the house.

I heard a terrible scream behind us. Charnock was following us, but his master had plunged back into the flame-filled attic room and was trying to seize something in his arms, something that glittered responsively in the leaping red light.

It was the miniature mountain of gold, reflecting the flames with a fiery copper-color dancing over its enticing surface.

"Yes, iron pyrites," said Sandys. "One of the commonest of ores—found everywhere. A beautiful golden color, lustrous, but quite worthless. Charnock and Henderson brought Sir Antony some, and pretended they had made gold, so that he would believe the experiment was progressing. He has come back to save it."

Almost as soon as he'd finished saying those words, we were out on the drive of Jesmond Place, Zaraband whinnying as the timbers of the old mansion cracked and flamed, the fire spreading from the attic beams with terrifying speed. There was no time for philosophical meditation on human greed. God help anyone still in the house; there would be no saving them.

"I'll go to the stables," I called. "There are horses there, and a groom who has quarters over the stalls."

But already we saw the fellow running round the side of the house to safety, holding the reins of two horses. One was the big animal from whose back the dying Cyriack had fallen. The other, to my surprise, I also recognized. A stumping, clumping old fellow, tagging along gallantly, his dappled coat almost white with age.

"Why, Dobbie!"

It was an animal from the Malfine stables, Belos's pony, whom I had once purchased from Lilian Westmorland's flinty-hearted uncle.

"Yes, I borrowed him," said Elisabeth, "and a snail-slow ride he was! I thought I should never get here."

"Never mind, you did get here in time." I squeezed her shoulder under the black silk cloak. "What a fool I was, to try to keep you at home out of danger!"

"Oh, you realize that now, do you?" There was a mocking look in her eyes. "Some women, Ambrose, are very disinclined to obey orders."

"And I shall never again attempt to issue them to you! Mind you, that was a difficult shot—between Charnock and myself. I didn't know you had such an excellent aim."

"I used to practice with my brothers in France," she called, as we all hastened out of range of the sparks and heat from the funeral pyre of Sir Antony's greed.

"But where are Clara Jesmond and Mrs. Romey?" I had to shout now, above the sound of the cracking beams, and the heat of the fire was burning my throat as I spoke, yet I could not but think of those two women, perhaps trapped and terrified in that inferno.

"No, Ambrose, no!" exclaimed Elisabeth. "They are safe. I have taken them to the inn." And she pulled me away as I turned to run toward the house.

Already I could see the massive tie-beams exposed and blackening as flames leaped along the roof. Jesmond Place would not survive much longer, and already there were small tongues of flame leaping through the air toward the stables. The groom had acted quickly, but nevertheless only just in time.

"There was naphtha in the crucible," said Charnock. "That was part of the . . . part of what Dr. Henderson taught me; one of the things I added. But there was more in a flask on the bench." As if to confirm his words, an almighty *bang* exploded from the upper windows of the house, and a great shower of sparks rained through the air.

What fools! Meddling with substances so dangerous, as if they were toys.

"We can do nothing to stop the fire now," said Sandys. "And Antony Jesmond's life is utterly lost."

"It was lost long before," said Charnock, with a shaft of insight I had not expected from him.

CHAPTER 22

A small procession was ready to make its way along the village street, one which no doubt was observed by many secret gawpers. The advance guard consisted of myself, Charnock, and a stout fellow with a cudgel, the groom from Jesmond Place, to reinforce the landlord of the Green Lion in his watch. I wanted to spare Elisabeth any further alarms, but she was running along close behind me and Sandys followed the party.

My purpose was to ensure that Henderson and Charnock were held responsible for their part in the fearful story. If they had not fanned the flames of Sir Antony's greed, he would not have neglected his wife, nor tried to suborn Kelsoe into working for him. Murder, they might not be directly guilty of: fraud, they had certainly committed. I intended to make sure they were both kept under guard till Sir Edward Knellys should arrive and deal with them. I looked forward to explaining Lady Jesmond's innocence to that sour dignitary.

But as we approached, I saw a strange sight. Something was glittering in the distance, at the end of the street. There was a kind of gilded flickering in the sunshine, as if something live and golden were fluttering in the wind, outside the dull gray stones of the alchemist's house. The plump landlord of the Green Lion, whom I had left on guard outside, was struggling with the rusty padlock on the door of Henderson's house.

Charnock gave an exclamation, and began running. I quickened my long-legged pace, my mind trying to make sense of what my eyes were seeing. The groom was lagging behind.

Hanging on the outside of the house was something white covered with flowing golden streamers, with tangles and knots of gold. This absurdly heavenly vision overlooked the glistening muddy creek, now full with the incoming tide, and seemed almost to have a dancing reflection in the mercury-colored water.

As I got closer, I saw what it was. An old man, with a white beard, covered in a great white feathered cloak, hanging from the bars of a window high above the ground. And the cloak was sewn all over with golden ribbons and trimmings that moved and rustled in the breeze. They gave an impression of life, but I looked up at the face, at the bulging eyes, and I knew the truth.

Henderson, in the last magician's guise he would put on.

Charnock gave a great howl of grief and ran frantically toward the house.

"Is that real gold, sir, on the cloak?" The groom had caught up by now and was gasping at the sight. The landlord had the door open, and was struggling with his stout bulk up the stairs.

The groom and I were close up. "Tinsel," I said. "Gold ribbons, gold thread—nothing of any substance. All tinsel."

We cut him down from the window from which he had hanged himself, and laid him in his room, still covered in the great cloak; the downy feathers stirred in the slight breeze, almost as if the form underneath it were still alive.

"He kept it folded away," said Charnock. "It belonged to old Thomas. My grandfather said a wizard could fly in that cloak. That's why they keep the church locked."

For a moment, I could not follow his train of thought.

"What church—oh, that one at Otterhampton? What has that to do with it?"

Charnock looked puzzled. "Didn't you know? He's buried there—old Thomas, my ancestor. There's no church at Combwich, apart from the one at Jesmond Place. After they buried him in Otterhampton, the church was locked and the rector keeps the key, only he doesn't live at Otterhampton anyway, and the church is opened only for a service on a Sunday."

I remembered the heavy lock on the door in the church porch.

"They keep it locked because . . . because people said he might fly out of it. Fly out of his grave and out of the church. They're not educated people, my lord, and there's been stories handed down ever since old Thomas came to live here. There's very few go to the services in the church at Otterhampton—and they come away as quickly as possible afterward."

And it had probably been easier for the rectors of Otterhampton to go along with the wishes of their flock. I remembered the sunny churchyard, deserted except for sheep of the woolly variety.

Young Charnock, descendant of that much-feared Thomas

who might have spread wings and swooped up out of the church, went on speaking, though his voice was still shaky.

"When Dr. Henderson came, he said he would fly away in that cloak one day."

Perhaps that had been the legendary source of the landlord's terrified inquiry; perhaps superstitions based on the alchemist's feathered cloak had lingered on.

"But it is terrible that Henderson should kill himself," and I looked at Charnock, and realized for the first time how young he was. Tears stood in his eyes. He was looking at me with a kind of bewilderment.

"I think he could not stand the humiliation," said I. "It was not just imprisonment he wanted to escape, but the demonstration that his magic was false and his alchemy mere fraud."

I saw that the young face was twisted up with grief; in all the world, Henderson had found at least one fellow human being who lamented him, had found that devotion not in Oxford where he had demonstrated his scientific brilliance, but buried here in the heart of somebody whom I could now see was still in many ways a village boy.

The landlady of the Green Lion had arrived to join the throng and was fluttering round in a state of agitation. "The ladies at the inn! They are right anxious."

"Oh lord, yes," exclaimed Elisabeth. "I had forgotten. They will be waiting for news!"

"Sandys, will you go on?" I asked. "I would like to know that cursed alchemical den is destroyed. There must be many poisons in that house which should be disposed of safely, lest they fall into the wrong hands."

"Very well, Malfine, I'll see that no more harm can come of it."

We hurried down the street, past the village houses. Covert observation from behind the cottage windows had been abandoned: here and there groups of people were emerging into the street, alarmed by the commotion. A woman protectively pulled her child into the deep folds of her skirt, staring down the street and shading her eyes to see what passed.

We found them in the parlor, both of them, seated at a table which bore a tray set with glasses and a decanter of something that looked like Madeira.

"Dreadful stuff," observed Elisabeth, as she seated herself, taking a sip and tossing her ringlets with the ensuing shock. "My papa would never have allowed such vinegar in his cellar!"

She placed the glass down upon the table.

"Your papa was a wine-merchant with a fine taste and a cellar worth a small fortune," I observed. "A country inn will never accommodate your palate."

These were our words, not betraying our relief at knowing each other thus alive, thriving, and even complaining.

I seemed to be acquiring some British reticence in matters of the heart. Instead, therefore, of taking Elisabeth into my arms and ascending the stairs to the nearest bedchamber, I uttered polite greetings to the other persons at the table.

Clara Jesmond looked as if she had been crying. The room went very quiet as I sat down next to Mrs. Romey.

"Ambrose," said Elisabeth, "last night when I arrived at Jesmond Place I could not find anyone—neither you nor Dr. Sandys, so I thought it better to get them out of there. There seemed to be something terribly dangerous in that house."

"You sensed danger, yet you went back?"

For a moment, there was no one but Elisabeth and myself in the dingy little inn parlor. It was a long look, that seemed to take us half a lifetime.

"Would you doubt me?" she spoke quietly. "But first, Clara can shed some light on that poor young physician's death, can you not, Clara? You only have to repeat what you confided in me last night."

Clara Jesmond was sitting opposite me. Her large blue eyes gazed unhappily at me and the blonde lace collar on her dress trembled with her nervousness, but I think she knew that she could go no further along the road of deceit. Things were simply too perilous for anything but the truth.

And the deceit, I reflected, as a ray of light came through the window and fell across both Clara Jesmond and Mrs. Romey, was not all with regard to Kelsoe. I turned my head in Elisabeth's direction, and saw a movement, just an acknowledgment. She had seen the same thing, perhaps earlier than I. But we must hear what Clara was prepared to tell us now.

"There was something further, Lord Ambrose. Something John Kelsoe must have written after that scrap which I showed you previously."

Clara Jesmond delved within a little velvet bag on a cord at her waist and produced a strip of paper closely covered with fine writing; without a word, she passed it over the table.

My darling: my existence is now a torture to me. I had believed you loved me, and would come away with me. And I thought you wanted me to act as I did in refusing to have anything to do with Henderson's schemes and contrivances. We don't need gold—false or real! We could have lived to-

gether, like two birds of the air, and I would have cared nothing—no, nothing for wealth or fame, so long as I had you with me. But you said you would not take me—and that, my love, my beautiful bird, is my death warrant. You want something I do not have—yet perhaps I can get it for you! Not now, not now, but after my death, some time when I am beneath the soil, it will happen. When that day arrives, think of me!

There was no signature, save an elaborate *J* crammed on to the end of the last line; I recognized it from the note which Kelsoe had left to Clara in their secret hiding-place.

I looked up from the small strip of paper on which Kelsoe had written his last words. "I found it in his writing-case," said Clara Jesmond. "He must have left it there before he . . ."

"There was no writing-case in his room!" I exclaimed.

Mrs. Romey leaned forward and said with sudden determination, "No, indeed! I took every scrap of paper away. There was no time to see what was written upon it—I took his case and everything, in case there was anything of my lady's in it."

"But this was the only personal thing, save some letters from his mother," added Clara Jesmond. "The rest was all his scientific papers."

"And that explains why you found no papers in his room. You see, he did commit suicide!" exclaimed Elisabeth. Her smoky citrine-yellow eyes turned toward the woman sitting next to her, and she gazed carefully at Clara Jesmond's face, as if she were reading a story written there. "You see, Ambrose, as we know, Kelsoe fell in love with Clara, and when she would not have him, he killed himself. This last note proves it, does it not?"

"Yes, it would certainly seem to, taken with the previous message," I said. "Lady Jesmond, these messages could have proved your innocence."

"But it would have meant making everything public! Oh, I could confess certain things to you in private, Lord Ambrose, but to give Knellys this proof of—"

Here there came a sudden interference. I had almost forgotten the presence of Mrs. Romey, who was also seated at the table. She sat upright, with a light gray cloak pulled round her, and spoke softly. "It would have meant that my pretty one would have to confess everything, that she and Dr. Kelsoe . . . had a fondness for each other."

Clara Jesmond sat back in her chair, and sighed. "You need not disguise it in such terms. Yes, as I told you before, we were lovers and he wanted us to be together forever."

"But you would have been very poor!" This was Mrs. Romey.

"Yes," said Clara softly. "We should have been poor." She traced a finger in a pool of wine which had got spilled on to the rough table-top. "Such a life would not have been for me." She looked up again, directly at me, and I experienced the heart-stopping gaze of those huge blue eyes. "You are aware of my character, Lord Ambrose. I am not a woman who would like to contrive and make do, never to appear in society, always to live in the poorest of circumstances. I simply could not have borne it.

"I tried to put it as delicately as I could, but yes, that was what I told him. But we spoke also of his work for my husband. I said that he had been foolish, to act as he did and refuse to take part in what Dr. Henderson was doing for my husband. I said that perhaps alchemy did work after all, and if so, my husband would soon be rich! And even if it did not, why, if John Kelsoe would only go along with it, would help with the experiments and so on, at least he could stay beneath our roof and we could continue as we were. But no, he would have none of that! He could not play at that charlatan's game! That was what he said. So there was only one thing left—he would have to leave Jesmond Place; after all, he could hardly stay after he had more or less called my husband a fool to be taken in by alchemy!"

"And that, of course, would have meant leaving you, which he could not bear to do. So the poor young fellow killed himself. Professor Daubeny was right after all, when he said in Oxford that it was possible that a man could swallow prussic acid and still have time to compose his deathbed! But was there not more to it than that? What does the note say? 'You want something I cannot have.' "

Lady Jesmond cast her eyes down and murmured, very softly, "Wealth—I think that was what he meant. Oh, I feel ashamed to say so, but I'm afraid it is the truth. I could never have lived in some wretched lodging-house."

"Lady Jesmond, at least you are honest," said I. "There are many who never admit to such a thing, who would swear to embrace passion in a cottage and be content with love in a garret. It takes a brave woman to say the truth."

"And to see into her own nature," added Elisabeth. "But there is something I do not understand. I meant to ask you, Clara, what the rest of that sentence meant: 'perhaps I can get it for you.' And then he says: 'not now, but after my death.' "

Clara Jesmond was trembling again, and Mrs. Romey got up and put her shawl around her mistress's shoulders. "Oh, but I am not cold," she said. "I am fearful. I do not know exactly what he meant, but I think it was something to do with Cyriack."

"I believe that is exactly what he meant," I said gravely. "I think John Kelsoe killed Cyriack Jesmond!"

The three women stared at me. "But Kelsoe died first," said Elisabeth. "Do you mean he didn't really die? That he somehow was still alive and went on to commit murder?"

There was a long moment, during which the talk of magic and sorcery of which we had heard so much these last few days must have been uppermost in their minds.

"Oh yes, he died. Cyriack followed him to the grave," I answered. "But Kelsoe had set a trap before he died. When I went to Oxford, I had a silversmith cut open Cyriack's hip-flask. Within it had been placed a capsule, designed to dissolve when, as was his inevitable custom, Cyriack asked for it to be filled with brandy. It was the boy's own flask, that was kept in his room when he was not at home. Once the poison had been placed within the flask, it was merely a matter of time. Cyriack would come down from Oxford, and at some point would no doubt go for one of his fast gallops, and drain the flask in his usual precipitate fashion. All Kelsoe had to do was to contrive the capsule—an easy enough matter for a doctor, for drugs are often administered in such a form—and secure it to the inside of the flask. A little heat soon fixed it deep within, so it could not float to the surface, perhaps to be noticed and spat out as soon as it touched Cyriack's lips."

"How horrible! What cold-blooded planning!" Elisabeth shuddered as she spoke.

"Yes," I answered. "But it was a kind of legacy, you see. A bequest to Lady Jesmond."

Clara Jesmond's face told me she had understood.

"Cyriack was my husband's heir," she murmured.

"Exactly. If he were disposed of, then you would come

into your own. There are no more heirs—unless you yourself were to bear a child. At any rate, the Jesmond estate would no longer fall to Cyriack, who was a thoroughly unpleasant young man unlikely to treat his stepmother with kindness. But you could not remarry—nor take a lover."

"Yes," cried out Mrs. Romey. "That infamous will!"

"If I were not faithful to my husband's memory, I would receive nothing." Clara Jesmond was speaking. "That was a provision of the will."

"You had to make a choice, did you not?" said Elisabeth. "You could run off with your lover to romantic poverty, or you could stay and enjoy the comfort of your position as Lady Jesmond. But you could not have both. You had to make a choice, and your decision was against love in a garret."

Clara Jesmond was nervous and trembling, but with a kind of defiance.

"And what good would it have been to go and live in wretchedness? We would have soon come to hate each other, I am sure! And his profession, his career as a medical man, that would have been in ruins also, for a doctor must be of absolute respectability, must he not? No, I gave him up!"

Well, that seemed the answer to the sad puzzles of death. Kelsoe must have expected his beloved to rejoice in his refusal to turn alchemist, and anticipated that she would share his bitter bread of poverty. When she refused, his brain contrived a twisted stratagem that, as he thought, would ensure his mistress had what she wanted above all things: not love, but money. A dead man did not kill Cyriack Jesmond: it was no ghost that did it. But he was killed by a man already dead.

CHAPTER 23

MALFINE, as usual, was our refuge. Jesmond Place was uninhabitable, a roofless ruin, still stinking of smoke, but Jesmond's household was only temporarily homeless. There was apparently a dower house, unoccupied since the death of Sir Antony's mother some years previously, which would be made ready for habitation.

What sort of life would Lady Jesmond lead in it? I could not imagine her enduring the kind of solitary existence that threatened: she was not a creature who could survive without some society.

Belos took over the organization of a commissariat at Malfine, so that the refugees could be catered for; he had persuaded Mrs. Granby, a woman from the village, to come and see to the cooking. Yet amid the household whirlwind he began to say something to me privately several times and I was conscious that he wanted to speak to me on something which had to remain unsaid until beds had been made up and warmed, a little dressed chicken sent up from the kitchens for the ladies and some cold beef and pickles for myself. This, of course, was after Pellers in the stables had fed, groomed and watered Zaraband, who was the love and torment of his life, done the same for the patient Dobbie/Barbary and Cyriack Jesmond's big hunter, and found a lodging for the groom from Jesmond Place.

And Sandys came riding up later, to report that he had cleared out Henderson's lair in Combwich. "I destroyed those nasty wax heads, and so forth, and poured the contents of the flasks away. Burned the hemlock and the poisonous fungi."

He carried a pile of tattered leather-bound books under his arm.

"But I rescued his books, Malfine. I did not wish those to be destroyed. He had some fine herbals. No harm lies in books, only in what we make of them. What shall we do with them?"

"I suppose rightly they belong to young Charnock, and he should have them eventually. But not yet. I have plans for him. I'll put them in the library here at Malfine in the meantime."

"Very well. Oh, by the way, my wife says that Mrs. Lawrence has already been delivered of a fine girl. It seems my services were not required!"

"Excellent—I'll send over some grapes and wine."

Elisabeth was inquiring with keen interest as to the name proposed for the infant.

"Well . . ." Dr. Sandys hesitated. "You know how horse-mad Sholto Lawrence is. He wanted to call his baby daughter . . . well, he wanted to call her Zaraband!"

I saw nothing preposterous in this, although Elisabeth fell into a chair with laughter.

"Oh lord, she's a *baby,* not a foal!"

"So she is to be called Florence, after my wife," said Sandys. "That is . . . there was some discussion between husband and wife, and the little girl is to be called Florence Zaraband!"

Now we were all reduced to laughter!

Well, we all have our fantasies! My "cakes of glass" were nigh as homely as "cakes of soap," no more than the lumps of glass cullet which Henderson had ordered, for the making of the alchemical vessels. So much for my imagination.

It was not till later that evening that Belos and I had an opportunity to speak.

He was uncommonly close about the matter, yet, as I discovered, there were two subjects on which there were disclosures to be made, one that affected him very closely, the other less so.

The evening was warm; the curtains had been left undrawn so that from the library I might look out on the vast sweep of the lawns, leading down to the great trees around the lake. The greens and blues of the day were fading to wraithlike misty grays, the branches black outlines against the gray. Lady Jesmond had been in an exhausted and distressed state, and she and Mrs. Romey had begged to retire early; Elisabeth was changing for dinner.

"It is time for some truth, my lord."

The serious tone in Belos's voice surprised me, and I began to have some forebodings.

The black cat, Cordillo, had followed him into the library and leaped on my knees, peering out of the window with his amber eyes.

"Truth, Belos? Are you sure?"

"My lord, I must tell you this; it came to me from a close friend. One whom I trust."

I was surprised at this. Since our return from Greece, Belos and I had lived in seclusion. I had not thought he had made any close friendships in the neighborhood; he went occasionally to the alehouse, it is true, but merely to pick up a little local gossip now and again.

"Well, I suppose I must bear it, if you really will not desist." But, looking at his face, I dropped my flippant manner and grew serious. The fur of the cat was warm and thick under my fingers.

"This information comes, my lord, from the . . . the person I met at Edmund Kean's funeral."

"The actor friend? I remember you mentioned him. An old comrade from the Theatre Royal in Bristol, was it not?"

"Yes, and I have been in correspondence with him since. A letter came while you were away at Jesmond Place. I have been expecting your return daily and did not wish to write to you there about this subject in case my letter should be intercepted."

"The puzzle becomes more and more intriguing, Belos. What did your friend have to say?"

"That he had heard a strange tale in the theater, my lord. You see, I had mentioned to him that you were intending to visit Sir Antony and Lady Jesmond. It seems that he heard that name again, from an elderly actor who was playing Polonius . . . my friend was Horatio."

He seemed pleased when I commented that his friend must be a success upon the boards, for Horatio was quite an important role.

Thou hast been
As one, in suffering all, that suffers nothing;
A man that fortune's buffets and rewards
Hath ta'en with equal thanks . . .

". . . And then something about 'Give me that man that is not passion's slave . . .' Is that not what Hamlet says to Horatio?"

"Yes, my lord. But what I have to tell you is not about Shakespeare—it is about an actress. I think that it is time for the whole truth to come out.

"It seems that Mrs. Romey was a very beautiful young actress at the Theatre Royal in Bristol, some twenty-five years ago, who left the stage because she had an illegitimate child, a daughter. That was the last piece in the puzzle, was it not? The father could not marry her, but he set her up in business as an inn-keeper, to make provision for her and the child."

Light was fading in the real world.

"Belos, yes, that accounts for many things!"

"If Clara Jesmond *is* Mrs. Romey's daughter . . ."

"Yes, I had already thought that might be the case. There is a physical similarity between them, but even more than that, Mrs. Romey has a clear and confident voice—and I recollect Miss Anstruther saying that Clara Jesmond was very apt at learning languages, so I suppose she has inherited some of her mother's ability to imitate accents."

I was turning toward Belos as I said all this, recollecting various small things that had transpired at Jesmond Place: the familiarity with which the housekeeper addressed her mistress, the way in which she had drunk from her cup. The unusual intimacy between Clara Jesmond and Mrs. Romey to which Sir Antony had so objected was explained as the natural affection between mother and daughter. Antony Jesmond had no doubt feared that if the housekeeper were treated like a member of the family, then the whole story of his wife's low background might come out.

Elisabeth had entered the room as we were speaking, and I added as she came and sat beside me, "I did think at one moment that the landlord's wife Naomi might have been the lady with the theatrical past."

"Goodness, Ambrose, what made you consider that possibility?"

"She had damned fashionable shoes."

Elisabeth looked pityingly at me.

"Oh, Ambrose. Their feet are the same size!"

This seemed a gnomic statement.

"No, I suppose you would not have noticed that. But it explains the connection between Lady Jesmond and the landlady. You still do not see the point? Clara Jesmond used to pass on her old shoes—and her clothes sometimes, as well. She is a kind-hearted woman."

She stopped suddenly and I saw that the door of the library was partly open, and a woman was standing there.

"Mrs. Romey—"

"I believe the lady's stage-name was Suzanna Bellinger," and Belos bowed to the erstwhile Mrs. Romey as she came hesitantly into the room.

"So you have found out our secret, Mr. Belos. Well, we could not keep it forever; indeed, I would not have wished to keep it at all, for I have no shame concerning my late profession. It was Sir Antony made Clara and me swear to keep it from the world, for he was ashamed of having a wife from such a background. He said all the gentry would consider it utterly disreputable and they would not receive Clara in any of their houses. We must hide the fact that she came out of an inn, let alone what had gone before. And he said I could live as their housekeeper—but I must know my place."

This was said with an edge of hatred which I could well excuse, remembering how ruthlessly Sir Antony had crushed any signs of affection which his "housekeeper" had shown to his wife.

The woman continued: "Of course, I could have stayed behind in the inn after their marriage, but he said that I would never see my daughter again, if I chose to do that. So I had to go with her to Jesmond Place."

"And will you remain silent about your past? You need not fear that we will expose your history, if you wish for secrecy still."

The woman shook her head. "No, my lord. I'll speak to Clara, but I think she will follow my inclination. Now that Sir Antony is gone, we have no reason to hide our past. In any case, Clara has never been accepted by the other county families; we would hear them murmur sometimes, about her lack of breeding, or her vulgar manners! It was so painful, when Sir Antony made us keep up that pretense in public—we were never permitted to acknowledge that she was my daughter. That was the hardest part I have ever had to play—and it seemed I would have to play it forever. Thank God it's all over."

As she went out, I saw a strange look crossing Belos's face.

"That is something I, too, wish to say."

"What, are you returning to the stage too? Are you planning to tread the boards again? Am I to lose my entire household to the damned theater?"

"No, my lord, I meant that I don't wish to play a part any more."

He walked across to the window so that I could not see his face and stood looking out as dusk was falling.

"Not just the role of your butler, my lord."

I had a presentiment of what was coming. Although he had

given no sign, no word, in all those long months when he had tended my wounds and run my household, yet I knew what lay unspoken there, in the evening, in that long library where the cases of gilded spines glimmered away into the darkness.

"My lord, did you ask yourself why I was in Greece?"

"No. Never!"

"But surely, you must have had some curiosity, some notion as to why—"

"As to why you came to be lying in a malaria-ridden Levantine attic, reciting *Hamlet* in your fever? What you were doing in Greece in the first place? Why you were beyond the reach of our particularly savage laws and our gross British moral hypocrisy? No, Belos, I most carefully did *not* ask myself those questions. And do not now answer them for me. Some other time in our friendship, I beg you."

"Very well, my lord. But I wish to return to Bristol."

"I understand that perfectly, Belos. I will not inquire your reasons for doing so; are they—are they connected with the person you met at Richmond?"

"Yes, my lord. I wish to be with him."

This was spoken very quietly, but with a clear determination and courage.

"I am sorry, Belos, that our household here at Malfine seems to be diminishing, but you have repaid any debt you owed me a thousand times or more."

"I should have died in Greece, if it was not for your lordship. I was sick and starving when you found me there."

"And I should have died of my wounds—or of my doctors' advice—had you not stopped them bleeding me and brought me home to tend me here. So our scores are even. You owe me nothing, Belos. Will you take anything with you? I can let you have funds."

"No, there is nothing I need from you, my lord. Let the boy, young Crawshay, have the pony; he is a quiet old beast and must live out his days in peace. He is no Barbary, after all!"

But there were tears in his eyes later on, and not, I am sure, an actor's fakes.

The black cat, Cordillo, was clinging to Belos's shoulder as he walked through the gates of Malfine the next day. I watched as his figure, clad in nondescript brown, grew smaller and smaller in the distance. Belos did not look back.

"Open up the house, Ambrose. The ballroom, your mother's rooms."

Elisabeth was behind me.

"It is time for an end to the old life."

I could see Belos no longer. I turned round to her.

EPILOGUE

"SO you'll take him?" I said.

Professor Daubeny nodded his head.

"You have persuaded me, Malfine, though I have some misgivings. The young man's qualifications for entry to Oxford are somewhat unusual."

"Yes, I fancy he knows nothing of whoring, nor of gambling—"

"I assure you Oxford is becoming a far more serious place than it was in your young day."

"Nor of psalm-singing, neither—"

"But I've talked to him," continued Daubeny, hardened by the irrelevant interruptions of a thousand undergraduates over the course of his long career, "and I find he has a little learning. He knows some natural science—something of many minerals and elements—and Henderson taught him Greek and Latin, and even Arabic science as well. We can build upon that, if we can clear all this alchemical nonsense about creating gold out of his head. It was a tragedy that Henderson went the way he did, but something can be salvaged, if we give this boy a chance."

Opening the door of his laboratory, Daubeny called out to the lad who was sitting on a wooden chair in the hall outside—a dark and solemn place, full of varnished wood and smelling of chemicals. Nervously, Charnock came in, his hair sticking up at the back of his head. Now it could be seen how young he was: no older than most of the students in Oxford, if the truth be known. The perverse training which Henderson had given to his mind, and the greedy demands which Sir Antony Jesmond had laid upon him, had made him seem older than his years.

"Now, young man," began the Professor, "Lord Ambrose and I have decided that we can enter you as a student here at Oxford, if you will apply yourself to serious study under my tuition."

There was a brightness in young Charnock's eyes that told us he was eager to begin. Yet he hesitated still, looking back and forth from Daubeny to myself, ruffling his hair with his hand, as he stood against a bench covered with retorts and tubes.

Daubeny sensed the difficulty.

"Come, young man. Lord Ambrose here has said that he will pay your college fees and living expenses, so that you can learn some rational science. What do you say?"

Charnock seemed suddenly to come to life.

"Oh, yes, sir!" he said. "Yes, please!"

He went out accompanied by Simon, Daubeny's apprentice, whose scholarly young face I remembered from my previous visit.

"One moment, Professor," said I.

I went out and slipped them a guinea apiece.

"Keep clear of Mother Louse, but an evening at the Blue Dog will do you no harm." Simon looked shocked, so I added hastily in my severest tones, "But you are to pay attention to your studies, mind, Charnock."

I think he will. What was there left for him in Combwich, after all? He had seen most of what he had learned there collapse in a heap of flaming rubbish. And he had learned too much to be content to remain there in the depths of the countryside, yet not enough to do aught else.

There is a well-known quotation: "A little learning is a dangerous thing." But people rarely go on to quote the next line: "Drink deep, or taste not the Pierian spring."

Oxford will give Charnock his chance to drink deep.

Well, we are a nation of soft-minded gulls who will believe in all sorts of nonsense from parsons and prestidigitators alike, but if Daubeny makes a rational man out of a sorcerer's apprentice, at least I shall have plucked one brand from the burning.